# 90 Days IN THE Pen

By

## G. L. Rasmussen

Cover Photo:

Thanks to Ed Prescott and Chester Southwick of Prescott Land &
Livestock at Jerome, Idaho. Chester Southwick, pictured.

1

G. L. Rasmussen

This is a work of fiction. Names, characters, and places are the products of the author's imagination or are used fictitiously and are not to be construed as real. Any resemblance to actual locales, organizations, or persons, living or dead, is entirely coincidental.

# 90 Days IN THE Pen

ISBN: 978-0-9846618-0-0

Printed in the United States of America

This book is dedicated to:

  Margie. Thanks for seeing me as a work in progress.

  The Idaho Writer's League. I'd still be rewriting if not for you.

  Loy Ann Bell, who began most phone calls to me with, "I don't want to be a whip-cracker, but . . ."

  The many friends and family that have chipped away at the rough edges. Mine and my writing.

  **90 Days in the Pen** is a compilation of personal and shared experiences, with an adequate amount of embellishment, from years in the saddle and just plain livin'.

Events that have been portrayed and may seem beyond belief are based in fact, witnessed by myself and/or others. Yes, bulls do march five abreast and some fools do return to work after being fired. Twice. Dogs get lost, never return and grow better in the memory.

I've owned some great horses and started too many fractious colts. Seven broke ribs, a hand and a foot, plus a punctured lung with accompanying x-rays to prove it. My fingers are all intact, though. I'll leave it to you to decide what that says about my roping skills. Or lack of.

Since I started writing, my wife has grown less fearful of receiving calls from the ER nurses and no longer has to ask, "What did he break now?"

Fizz (Panda) is gone. As is Pup one, two and three and Dog. Zip (Bonehead) resides in the corral, under worked and overfed.

At one point in the writing of this book, I toyed with the idea of getting into Fizz's head because he has such a strong personality. I tried it once, enjoyed the outcome and ran with it. No offense intended to those that *didn't* sleep through POV (Point of View) 101.

## Table of Contents

"Pretendin' ta be the runt is worse than
pretendin' ta be the tall hog at the trough."

G. L. Rasmussen

G. L. Rasmussen

# Prologue

*Howdy, Journal: May 2*

*We're almost to the Sprocket spread. Fizz hopped out of the truck, took one look around and peed on the directional sign. I get the feeling my dog ain't real taken with this place.*

*After stayin' a night in Elko, Nevada, we'll make the final pull to the ranch. A couple cowboys from an outfit in Ruby Valley noticed the California plates. They set me up with a pen and hay for my horses at the fairgrounds. They know the gal that runs the place.*

*We went and got a steak and then shot the breeze 'til closing time. Rick is from Cottonwood, Arizona. Trace is a local boy. They said if things didn't work out where I was headed, look 'em up.*

*Left Elko at first light. There's still some nip in the morning air, enough that the horses looked like fire-breathers. I've turned off Great Basin Highway for the final two hours of the drive, but I decided to pull over to write a bit, maybe do some sketches. Don't know how long before I'll get back this way.*

*Bare grey hills stretch to the horizon. Seems like another planet compared to my last place. Storms came off the Pacific almost ever' day and kept the cows up to their bellies in grass. Crossways Ranch is a good outfit; I just needed a change of scenery.*

*I thought about droppin' a fishing line in this reservoir here, but it's gettin' hot. The fish are probably sittin' in front of an air conditioner having a cold drink anyway.*

*It's near ten years since I high-tailed it outta Oregon. I've been to some places I could only dream about had I stayed. My folks worry that I'll just drift and Grandpa calls me "Tumbleweed." They ain't getting it. I got too much in me to stand still. I figure I'll know when it's time to roost.*

# One
## WELCOME TO SPROCKET, INC.

The rancher hitched his thumbs in his belt and looked straight at Scoot. "You're fired."

"You hired me not five minutes ago, Mr. Sprocket."

"Oh, are you the new pen rider? I'm T.F. Sprocket. I own the place. Have you met the foreman, yet? Where is Red?"

"I'm right here and my name ain't Red. It's Wil."

T.F. looked from Scoot to Wil. "So who's Red?"

"You fired him a few years back."

"I liked Red."

Scoot shrugged. "Why did you fire him, then?"

"He got on my nerves."

Wil pulled off his hat and swatted at a horse fly. "I'm going to show this guy around the place. You ought to get out of the sun, T.F."

"Great, why don't you show him around the place. Oh, you're both fired," he said, pointing a gloved

11

finger at them as they climbed into a ranch truck. Scoot's dog had just finished relieving himself on the old man's tires. T.F. glared at him.

Fizz sat on his tail and glared back. *I'm new here and just marking my territory. That truck belongs to me now.*

"You're fired too," T.F. told him.

Scoot glanced out the back window. "Seems like a regular occurrence around here."

"Yup, and unless I say otherwise, keep coming to work. T.F. takes good care of us, but at 73, he's starting to slip a few cogs."

Scoot got the lightning tour of T.F. Sprocket Land and Livestock before being introduced to the rest of the crew.

"Boys, this is our new feedlot rider, Scoot Merritt." Everyone gave him a nod of acknowledgement.

"Over there is Tink, the token Navajo, as he calls himself. This is Buck. That's the Clegg brothers, Matt and Cody. Bronc here is the ranch manager and that's also a Buck. He's a Harmstead, the other's a Turnbow."

Scoot shook hands all around. "Where can I stow my bedroll, Wil? I might as well git ta work."

"I'll show you to the penthouse suite. Whatever the schedule was at your last outfit, we start at four in the a.m. here."

"Great, I get to sleep in."

- - # - -

*Howdy, Journal. Made it!*

*Finally met Wil, the feedlot foreman. We'd only talked over the phone. He hails from Colorado. Got interviewed by the owner, who hired me, fired me and then fired me again. T.F. is gonna keep things interesting. One minute he's all there and the next he ain't. I'm pretty sure he fired Fizz but the dog didn't seem too put out.*

*Got introduced to the other hands. They fit the place. Then I moved into my living quarters. It's bigger than a pup tent, a mite smaller than Trump Towers.*

G. L. Rasmussen

# Two
## A'horseback in the Sprocket Outback

Fizz sat on the truck bed watching the ranch dogs circle each other, growling and snapping. *Have at it, boys. I already cleaned up the scraps.*

The crew saddled in the dark while their stomachs tried to figure out what to do with the biscuits and gravy that Callie, the ranch manager's wife, fed them for breakfast. Biscuits in an oil slick seemed more like it.

T.F. appeared under the yard light and gave the orders for the day. "I want you boys to gather everything from Rustler's Creek on south and push 'em to Cold Springs. We'll sort out the commercials, stick those in the pens, then drive the ranch cattle to summer pasture."

He kicked at one of the dogs. "You mutts git it over with so we can go to work." The dogs fought for a couple of minutes, then slunk off to their respective porches to wait for the call to load up. "Your wife's gotta quit feeding them dogs, Bronc. Just puts 'em in a surly mood."

Bronc stopped saddling his horse. "It don't do much for me either, boss."

T.F. rubbed his stomach. "Any of you boys know how to cook?"

Everyone took a sudden interest in his own boots.

- - # - -

About the time the sun lit the far hills, the caravan of ranch trucks and stock trailers descended into the valley where Rustler's Creek began. There was very little talk except for the rumbling of queasy guts.

Buck downshifted to pull the final hill before Rustler's Creek. "I'm going to start grazing with the horses. I can't take much more of that woman's cooking,"

"It do keep ya regular," the other Buck replied.

The hands had unloaded, paired up and were riding off in various directions while Bronc shouted his version of T.F.'s orders.

Tink and Scoot continued down the canyon. They had just chased half a dozen yearlings out of some willows lining the small stream when Tink hopped off his horse and ducked behind some sagebrush to unload the morning's fare.

"I know it's not the cowboy way to shoot the cook, but I'm gonna make an exception." He wiped his mouth on a sleeve.

"It may not be the cowboy way, but do Navajos have a rule against shooting the cook?"

Smiling, he swung up into the saddle, "Nah, Scoot, we've never had a problem shooting you white eyes, no matter what your profession."

The cattle walked single file up a game trail that led to the top of the plateau. Scoot and Tink could feel the temperature change the higher they rode. Some momma cows with calves nursing at their sides moved in the opposite direction when the cowboys came into sight.

It would be another hot, cloudless day. The high desert had its own unique beauty, especially at first light. The purple cast on the distant peaks would turn to gray as the sun rose higher. The yearlings that the two picked up at the base of the bluff started running and kicking up their heels when they spotted the other cattle.

Scoot and Tink followed the herd, checking draws as they went. When the cattle bunched up at one of the stock ponds, the cowboys left them and turned south toward another of the tanks.

By noon they had nearly three hundred grazing at the northern-most point of the plateau. While Scoot tentatively sniffed the lunch that'd been packed for them, he noticed that his partner had tossed the sandwiches on the ground and was chewing on some beef jerky from his saddlebag.

"We ain't supposed to eat that stuff. It's for killin' coyotes." He handed Scoot the bag of jerky. They sat and ate, watching the cattle graze.

"Is Tink a Navajo name?"

"Naw. My real name is Benjamin. My father was a railroad man and would be gone for weeks at a time, working long hours. He couldn't figure out why I didn't want to do the same. He kept telling me I wasn't gonna be worth a 'tinker's damn' if I didn't figure out where I was going in life. Tink stuck. How about 'Scoot?'"

"Nope, it ain't Navajo, neither. I got it from a guy I worked for that figured I didn't move fast enough. He was a little like T.F. only firin' on all eight."

They bunched the herd and started in the direction of Cold Springs. Mustangs watched them from a nearby hilltop and then continued grazing.

The cattle were strung out and moving in the direction of the gathering area as the day began cooling down.

The water at Cold Springs had been fenced off, so they let the herd filter through the gate to get a drink and mother up. Dust spirals to the west announced the arrival of more cattle.

T.F. raced up to the mounted horsemen in his flat bed truck, slid to a stop and tossed off bedrolls and a cooler. He had decided they would camp for the night and sort first thing in the morning.

"I'll be back as soon as I find Bronc. He got lost again."

Buck H. twisted in the saddle. "We ain't seen him since he chased a couple mavericks off Table Top."

T.F. gunned the truck and disappeared in a cloud of dust. Half an hour later, he pulled up next to where the bedrolls and food lay. "Hey, Scoot, gimmee a hand with this water."

Scoot dismounted and reached for the cooler.

"You okay, T.F.?"

"Yeh. Bronc's horse dumped him in the middle of a cactus bed. I ain't never been comfortable pullin' quills out of another guy's butt." He jumped into the truck and vanished into the growing shadows. Scoot told the other hands what T.F. had said.

Bronc finally rode in later and dismounted very carefully.

"You look a little sore," Tink said, with a half grin.

"Me and the horse covered some rough ground so I decided to take it easy on him the last few miles."

"Have a seat and take a load off." Scoot offered, trying to hide a smile.

"Naw, I need to stand for a while."

- - # - -

Hobbled horses cropped at the small bunches of grass on the shadow side of the bluff. Dropping behind the mountains, the sun colored the clouds fire-orange while a dark blue sky began revealing stars.

Cody Clegg peeked into the food cooler. "She made roast beef sandwiches and threw in some store bought cookies. It's awful hard to screw that up." He noticed that everyone waited until he took a bite.

"What am I, the royal food taster?" Cody gasped and flopped onto the ground.

His brother, Matt, reached into the cooler. "Let's eat. He got the poisoned one."

Buck T. had a campfire blazing and a coffee pot sitting on a rock next to it when Bronc started singing songs about himself. The rest had settled onto the tree stumps that doubled for seats and talked over the day.

Tink unbuckled his chinks and laid them across a log. "Ya know, there's something about gettin' wore out on the trail. Sweat, dust and sore muscles make a man."

Grunts of agreement came from around the fire.

"I do miss my mattress though," Buck H. said.

More grunts of agreement.

"Did I ever tell you boys about the time I was on the Tonight Show recitin' my poetry?" Bronc asked. "Jay Leno commenced to crying and told me he could feel what it was like to be a cowboy."

"Do one for us." Matt winced, wondering why he had asked.

*"Bronc is my name,*
*Ridin' wild broncs is a game,*
*They buck high as the sky,*
*Trying to kill me, but I won't die,*
*That's why they call me Bronc."*

"You got any more?" Buck asked.

"Yeh, but I'm still working on 'em."

"How much you got wrote?"

"*Bronc is my name.*"

"Oh."

A few snores could be heard as the fire burned down and the cool of the desert settled on the group.

Tink glanced at Scoot. "Whatcha writin' in that little book?"

"Just making notes about the layout of the place."


- - # - -


*Howdy, Journal. Day 2*

*Covered a lot of ground today. Couldn't call it "pretty" though. Maybe "uniquely homely." Tink is a good hand. He was raised in Tuba City, Arizona and rodeoed in high school and college. He's smart as a whip. Keeps to hisself unless it suits him otherwise.*

*A band of mustangs with near 40 horses roam the place. Gotta include a colored drawing of them. Bronc got piled onto some cactus. Didn't shut him up though. That boy flat loves to hear himself talk.*

*We're sleepin' out in the open tonight. Don't mind it 'til some critter crawls in bed with me, then I might. There's a full moon coloring everything with that blue-white light. Frank Tenney Johnson was a master at night paintings. His cowboy sittin' a white horse and*

21

*lightin' a smoke is my favorite. Makes me wanna take up oil painting.*
*I imagine Fizz is gettin' to know the home place back at headquarters. He probably marked his territory and then hunted cats.*

- - # - -

Scoot closed the book, slid it into his saddlebag and watched the moonrise until he dozed.

# THREE
## AIN'T GOT THE SQUIRTS, YET

The moon hadn't moved much in the night sky when T.F. drove up to the corrals, slapping the truck door and yelling, "Breakfast's on. We're burnin' daylight."

"Daylight? That sure looks like the moon to me," Tink groused while he shook out his boots before pulling them on.

They washed down the greasy egg and bacon sandwiches with plenty of coffee and complaints.

"You won't come across anything else edible for a while," T.F. remarked.

The Clegg brothers roped and painted an "X" on the most promising bull calves while the others sorted the remainder of the herd. Tink and Scoot bunched the ranch stock and began pushing them towards Settler's Hole, the summer range. Another cloudless sky greeted them. The herd lined out in an easterly direction while a few calves tried to nurse their mommas from behind at a walk.

Ranch mornings are full of anticipation, but as the sun moves higher, the anticipation evaporates like the dew. A trail turned toward a small stand of aspen, then north.

Tink asked Scoot if he wanted a drink from the spring on the far side of the trees. The two hands entered the coolness of the grove where both horses dropped their heads and began munching on the sweet grass surrounding the small pool.

"Is the water any good?"

"I've been drinking it for most of a week and I ain't got the squirts yet."

They drank their fill, replaced the warm water in their canteens then mounted and trotted after the herd.

Summer pasture lay in a small valley with ample meadow and shade. The ranch bulls that had been dropped off the week before walked out of some quakies at the far end of the valley and came toward the herd. Tink and Scoot turned west to check one of the spring-fed tanks.

A cow with a bad hip and her new calf had settled in the grass around the spring. The fresh tracks of several deer and a coyote could be seen in the mud.

Scoot stood in the stirrups and scanned the area. "My grandpa, dad and I used to hunt in a place just above Grandpa's ranch that looked a whole lot like this. I remember one dry fall we hadn't seen a single deer, so we sat on some rocks on a ridge and ate our lunches.

"We musta talked for a couple hours about past hunts and other used-to-be's. Then everybody started gathering trash and picking up guns and packs when I hucked a big ol' rock into a stand of scrub oak. You should have seen it, Tink. The place exploded with deer, all of them bucks.

"We turned into the Keystone Cops, grabbing at each others gun straps, falling down and jumping up, then getting' knocked down again. By the time we got things sorted out, every one of them whitetails had disappeared over the ridge. There wasn't one shot fired. All three of us just stood there, stunned. Then we got to laughin' so hard it took another half hour to get our breath." Scoot sighed. "Those deer were probably just over the ridge laughing at us, too. Whatta a great hunt."

- - # - -

*Howdy, Journal*

*Told Tink about a huntin' trip with Dad and Grandpa. I do miss those days and their company. I did a quick sketch of deer flyin' over a far ridge. I favor those reds, oranges and browns against that electric blue, fall sky. Only problem is: It's still Spring. Can't wait to get back to my two-room mansion and put color to this. Dropped off some cattle in a nice little valley with lotsa water. Plenty of feed for most of the summer and bulls to put a twinkle in the cow's eyes.*

G. L. Rasmussen

# FOUR
## ARE YE WANTIN' TA DANCE A WEE SCOTTISH JIG?

Back at the ranch for a hot meal and fresh mounts, everyone learned that Bronc's wife had turned up pregnant and couldn't stand the smell of her own cooking. T.F. hired a replacement.

The food and the dog's temperaments improved immediately. So did the cowboy's grooming habits. Ruby, the new cook, was awful easy on the eyes and the crew took to hanging around the back door of the cook shack. T.F. decided that Ruby was a distraction and had gone to fire her several times, but since she was his sister's girl, and she'd stuff a warm oatmeal and raisin cookie in his mouth whenever he opened it, he just never quite got the job done.

It became obvious that Ruby's menu was hitting the spot.

27

"I swear, if you boys put on any more weight, all my horses are gonna be swaybacked by the end of summer," T.F. hollered one morning.

"They already were swaybacked when I hired on," Scoot said. "Besides, I noticed that your belt buckle's disappeared under that new addition, T.F."

"Have I fired you today, Scoot?"

"Yup".

"Well, you're fired again, 'cept don't pack your belongings 'til the work's done."

"Sounds like you're getting' sweet on me, T.F."

"Get to work, dang you. My grandpa moves faster and he's dead."

Nicholas (Nick) Sprocket, a fourth generation rancher and 'dyed-in-the-wool' Roosevelt man dubbed his only son, "Theodore Franklin". Having no political leanings, his son shortened it to "T.F."

The Sprocket clan emigrated from the highlands of Scotland. Angus McSprockett, T.F.'s great, great, great grandfather, dropped the "Mc" and one of the "t's" and settled in the Appalachians.

Not long after, the Sprockets got into a feud with the McDingall clan. What started as a shooting feud had to be scaled back.

"Haggus McDingall," Angus said, "what say we just beat on each other with fists? I'm running out of gunpowder and kin."

"It's a deal, Angus. Send over your woman and mine'll meet her halfway. Last one standing ain't gotta fix the fried squirrel and possum innards."

Once the fun had gone out of feuding, Angus pulled up stakes and headed to California. On a layover in Nevada Territory, he became interested in a pastime called "poker." Figuring Angus as an easy mark, the locals offered to let him in on a game.

"We'll teach ya how, friend, but ya gotta throw in a bit o' money just to make it interesting."

Those good ol' boys ended up leaving town in just their boots and the Sprockets were in the ranching business. Life had suddenly taken a turn for the better. Angus knew his way around cattle and, being Scottish, knew how to hang onto a dollar. Before long, they were big-time ranchers. Angus decided to make a run for mayor. He was generally liked and most folks would have voted for him, except for one problem: they didn't want a mayor named after a cow, so he changed his name to Wilson Sprocket and won hands down.

Towards the end of his term, he toyed with the notion of politicking on a larger scale and ran for territorial judge. Danged if he didn't win that, too.

Then Judge Sprocket wore a Scottish kilt to the town's Fourth of July celebration.

"Are ye wantin' ta dance a wee Scottish jig?"

An awkward silence followed, until somebody shot him through the bagpipes and the party continued.

Missus Sprocket never remarried, the kids went on to become lawyers, hotel owners and such, but no one ever wore a kilt. At least not in public.

The Sprocket spread survived the taming of the wild west, recessions, depressions, world wars, range wars, desperadoes, stampedes, bad cooking, revenuers and outhouse pranks. The family cemetery grew, but so did the ranch.

Today, headquarters rests in a mile-wide sheltered valley with spring-fed meadows dotting the valley floor. Five small homes, two single-wide trailers and a bunkhouse are backed up by a hill and built so close to each other that the occupants of one residence couldn't sneeze without the occupants of the others knowing it. The feedlot was downwind.

T.F.'s big ol' log home sat on a hill overlooking the whole valley. 87,000 acres of deeded range and 150,000 acres of grazing permits made it possible for 5,000 cattle, innumerable coyotes and assorted critters and Sprocket Land and Livestock to scratch out a living.

- - # - -

*Howdy, Journal: A Day Off*
  *Kinda liking the spot where the main part of the ranch sits. Fizz has been exploring and keeps himself occupied when I'm out gathering cattle, but he's always good help at the feedlot. I'd sure like to know what he's thinking sometimes. He's taken to Ruby and follows her around like a lovesick pup. Don't know if it's her or the cooking, but if I need to find him, I just hunt up Ruby. She talks fishin' as good as anybody. I need to unpack my gear.*

**30**

# FIVE
## A BULL NAMED "DOZER"

Scoot, Wil and Fizz left Sprocket ground just after first light, in a flatbed truck with a fifth wheel stock trailer. They passed the Goode Range Bulls Ranch sign out on the main highway a bit before noon. "There's a Great Bull and Then There's a Goode Bull," it said. Beneath the slogan hung a bleached-out skull with horns still attached and strips of hide that flapped in the breeze.

Scoot pondered the sign for three or four miles while watching for the turnoff to the ranch's main entrance.

"Hey, Wil, I know what that sign's 'sposed to mean, but if I was to say to you, "I'd rather buy a good bull than a great bull," what would you say?"

"Before I threw you outta the truck at seventy or after?"

"You choose."

"Okay. I'd tell you that old Chester Goode's son, Melvin, came up with that slogan and Chet's been proud of that beer hound ever since. I already tried explaining to them that it's all bass ackwards and 'fore I knew it I was in a Bubba forest. Chet, his five boys and what's been rumored to be a gal, C.J., were standin' over me about to wrap a brandin' iron around my head. I've loved that slogan ever since."

Scoot rubbed his chin. "I'm startin' to see the genius in it."

They turned off the main highway into the ranch, crawling past a paintless wood frame house.

Mrs. Goode stood in the backyard beating a rag rug. Her eyes followed Scoot and Wil as both Sprocket hands waved. She just kept beating on the rug like she had a grudge against it, her swing reminiscent of Babe Ruth punching homers into the parking lot.

The office turned out to be another paintless drab grey house surrounded by bull pens. A squeeze chute, attached to one pen, opened out into the yard surrounding the house. Luke Goode, the youngest, had the truck and trailer back up to a loading corral and then led the two cowboys to the office. Chet bragged on this year's crop of Black and Red Angus, Hereford and Gelbvieh while the paper work got sorted out.

Grabbing a ski pole out of the corner, Mr. Goode opened the door. "Let's go get T.F.'s bull." They proceeded down the alleyway toward the main pen. "You boys stay here and I'll bring your bull."

Ted, the oldest Goode son, slapped Scoot on the back. "You ain't gonna believe this."

Chester Goode came marching around the corner like a drum major leading a band, arms extended from his sides and ski pole in his left hand. Five Black Angus bulls walked abreast right behind him. The procession strutted past the astonished Sprocket hands and adoring Goode sons.

Luke elbowed Scoot. "Ain't that sumptin'? Hell, there oughtta be jets flyin' over."

The parade continued right into a pen and then the old man shut the gate behind him. Once the Sprocket bull was cut out of the herd and run into the squeeze chute, the processing began.

Wil heated the electric branding iron with the "Diamond TF." Scoot and Luke gave the yearling its shots and checked the vaccination tattoos and tags. Between the parade and processing though, something changed. Instead of simply trotting to the pen where the Sprocket trailer waited, the yearling exploded.

First on its 'get even' list were Scoot, Wil and Luke. Scoot and Wil topped the chute in one jump; Luke *almost* reached the alley fence. The Sprocket bull helped him over. Then it pulled up and surveyed the battlefield. Ted was whimpering and trying to claw his way up the Chinese Elm next to the office. It pawed the ground, blew snot and tossed Ted into the tree.

Chester Goode had hunkered down behind the table next to the squeeze chute. The bull might have passed him by, except for a quivering ski pole that pointed at the sun. The Angus hit the drum major's hiding place like a horn section run amuck. "GIT BACK!

33

BACK! HEEL! OLE! HEEELLLPP!"

Just when the table had almost been turned into splinters, C.J. ran out of the office, push broom in hand, yelling "HEY, STUPID." C.J. quickly changed direction in mid-stride and had been attempting to lock the door when the Angus ripped it off its hinges and carried the door and C.J., screaming, through the opposite wall.

"Does that scream sound like a guy or a gal, Scoot?"

"Gal."

"Well now we know."

It would have made short work of C.J. if not for her mother lumbering in their direction waving her rug beater. The bull put crosshairs on her ample behind and charged.

"Geez, Wil, we gotta end this 'fore that bulldozer kills somebody." Scoot whistled for Fizz.

The Aussie jumped out of the truck window and sprinted toward the whistle. "Sic 'im," Scoot shouted, pointing at the bull. Fizz put it in high gear, passed "Dozer" and was bearing down on Mrs. Goode's ham-sized calf.

"No, the bull!" Scoot hopped up and down, pointing at the correct target with both hands. Fizz adjusted his course and barking, brought the Angus back toward the office and then stopped.

An Australian shepherd is adept at mind games. They have the ability to "psych out" a thousand pounds of beef on the hoof, sending it retreating while wetting down both legs. This one was no match for Fizz. Pawing, shaking its head and snorting meant nothing to the dog, whose demeanor said, *Run while you can 'cause I'm gonna be all over you like a buzz saw.*

"Dozer" got the message and retreated toward the office. "Bring 'im, Pup!" Scoot shouted from the loading pen and then sprinted to the trailer. Fizz adjusted the Angus's trajectory. Wil stood behind the open door while Scoot played traffic controller and motioned the running bull into the trailer. A humbled Angus stood and shook at the front of the fifth wheel while the dog barked and Wil slammed the trailer gate shut. Leaning against it, he took off his hat and wiped sweat on a sleeve. Glancing at each other, they started laughing.

Wil caught his breath first. "I guess 'Dozer' fits, don't it, Scoot?"

The Goodes wandered around the yard, looking for casualties and a ladder to get Ted out of the tree. Scoot didn't know what possessed him to do it, but he waved to them as they pulled out and said, "You folks have a nice day."

- - # - -

*Howdy, Journal: Went for a drive*
*        Picked up a yearling bull for T.F., today. It tried to tear down Chet Goode's ranch and kill me and Wil in the process. It's as cranky as T.F. is most days.*

G. L. Rasmussen

# SIX
## THE GERM BUCKET

When one of the ranch trucks came up for sale, Scoot decided to get rid of the "germ bucket." The old GMC had been reliable even though it was "ugly as a hundred-miles of bad road." The object of his affection became a newer ¾-ton Ford flatbed. He wasn't picky about what he drove as long as it had some life left in it.

T.F. opened and closed the door a couple times. "A feller needs a respectable outfit to drive. It reflects well on him and makes for a good first impression."

"So why did you hire me when I pulled up in my tetanus wagon?"

"I figure anybody can make a mistake once in a while. Besides, Wil vouched for you, the trailer was packin' good-looking cow horses and my dogs liked ya. If you'd pulled up in that thing and tried to unload an Arab, I'd a shot you on the spot."

Scoot knew what Fizz was thinking by the

expression on the dog's face. Fizz gave the old truck one last look. *Shoot him anyway. He made me ride in this hunk-a-junk.*

"I'll keep that in mind, T.F. Let's shake hands on this truck of yours. I'm just gonna give mine to some teenaged kid since nobody in their right mind would pay good money for it."

Scoot decided to write a poem about his ex-truck. He titled it, 'The Germ Bucket.'

*My rigs a peatry dish on wheels,*
*It's a '74 GMC.*
*I'd recommend a current tetanus shot though,*
*If you're gonna to ride with me.*

*Probably oughta have hepatitis, too,*
*Get both A and B,*
*And try to find an Ebola vaccine,*
*If you're sure you want to ride with me.*

*The dog stays in the back of my truck,*
*He'll ride in the cab, reluctantly.*
*The only clean spot is the glove box,*
*Fizz really hates to ride with me.*

*I've often thought of cleaning my truck,*
*I just have one fear, you see,*
*I'd awaken a plague that destroys mankind*
*Wouldn't want that blamed on me.*

*Otherwise, it runs real good,*
*Oil was changed just recently,*
*The rubbers fair all around,*
*And that's a new air freshener pine tree.*

*I just had it inspected, too,*
*Though the mechanic was queasy,*
*He just looked at it through his shop window,*
*Signed the form and said, "This one's free."*

*So what do you think of this classic, sir?*
*There's not much more to see,*
*The sign says a 'thousand dollars',*
*You can have it for eight-fifty.*

*He wouldn't even take it for a spin,*
*Just walked away nervously,*
*You'd think folks would appreciate,*
*A guy with some honesty.*

T.F. would be taking two hundred dollars a month out of his paycheck for the next couple of years. Scoot could probably count on a job until the truck was paid off.

It also expanded Scoot's hunting and fishing range. He discovered an out-of-the-way lake near Padre Mountain that the Fish and Game stocked with trout. Tink, Ruby and he started making regular trips there. Not only could Ruby cook, but she knew how to fish. Plus, she was good company that could pack a picnic basket.

Fizz had grown quite fond of her and considerably fatter.

Sitting on the edge of a lake had a cleansing effect. The armor that one wore to keep out the rest of the world got shed and a different person emerged. In the weeks they spent fishing, the three became friends with a familiarity they protected.

What got shared on the lake stayed on the lake. Seems Ruby got expelled from a fat camp for kids after she broke into the kitchen and ate a whole cake. Tink's marriage and Scoot's weekend in jail for "stealing" his own horse were never discussed after tackle boxes were packed and loaded in the truck.

- - # - -

*Howdy, Journal: Finally, A Day Off*

*Drove up to Lost Lake today with Ruby, Tink and Fizz. The fish were keepin' their mouths shut. Probably 'cause we were doing too much talking. When the action gets slow, we start remembering our favorite fishing holes.*

*Fizz chased a whitetail fawn over the top of us. The little thing looked as surprised as we were. Its momma must have caught up to Fizz because he made a beeline back to camp and jumped on the bed of the truck. Glad he didn't find a bear cub.*

# SEVEN
## TINK FACES HIS PAST

Tink leaned forward in the saddle, crossed his arms and rested them on the horn. He had been watching the blue Dodge truck since it turned off the highway and slowly churned up dust in his direction. The outfit looked vaguely familiar but it wasn't until he saw the Arizona plates that he realized Leroy Whitehead had found him.

It idled to a stop; the driver rolled down the window and took off his chrome sunglasses. "I got a whippin' for a no good Navajo that ran off without leaving a forwarding address. You wouldn't know anything about that, would you?"

Tink grinned. "We don't hire Injuns here." He slid off his horse when LeRoy jumped out of the truck and wrapped his friend in a bear hug.

"When did you get back from Iraq? And who's that good looking young woman in the front seat?"

LeRoy walked around to open the door for her.

"Let me rephrase that. Who's that pregnant, good looking young woman with you?"

"Tink, this is my wife Rachelle. Rachelle, this is my best friend, Benjamin Williams."

"I'd like to give you a hug, too, but I've kind of got something in the way. Would you settle for a kiss on the cheek for now?" she asked.

Tink leaned forward and gently hugged her shoulders. "I will and it's a pleasure to meet you."

The two friends had been inseparable and were teammates in high school rodeo. Tink edged LeRoy out of the standings and went on to win the state all-around title. LeRoy continued to be a constant supporter and coach.

"College and the Marines put a lot of miles and years between us, didn't it Ben?"

"Last I heard, you were on your second tour training chopper pilots over there. Is LeRoy Junior gonna keep you stateside?"

"Well, that's partially why we came ahuntin' you. We'll be away for a bit. You know how us Whiteheads are."

The Whitehead family had a history of military men. LeRoy's grandfather had been a decorated soldier as a "code talker" during WWII. His father retired from the army as a Sergeant Major and now Warrant Officer LeRoy Whitehead continued the tradition as a Blackhawk helicopter pilot.

The cook shack began emptying out and Tink introduced his visitors to them. Even T.F. came over to shake hands and then instantly fired Tink for the rest of the day.

"Be back tomorrow afternoon when the trucks come in and you can have your job back."

- - # - -

*Howdy, Journal: June 22*
*I think it's somebody's birthday today, but I can't remember whose. Tink had some visitors, his best friend LeRoy from Tuba City and wife. They're moving to Hawaii before LeRoy heads back to Afganistan. He's a pilot. Wonder if there's any cow outfits in Hawaii?*
*When I worked at the Crossed T near Winslow, I sold two of Biscuit's pups to some folks on the reservation. Alvin, their son, invited me to the place. I must have looked lost 'cuz a female reservation cop pulled over and checked on me. She knew who I was (Alvin told her to be on the lookout for a confused cowboy) and had me follow her. She was related to him somehow.*
*They liked my dogs 'cause they were smart on sheep and stayed away from the coyotes. Spent the rest of the day learning about the Navajo's beginnings. Their family lines run back to the dawn of time.*

G. L. Rasmussen

# EIGHT
## ALL SHE WANTS IS TO HEAR YOUR VOICE

The three talked late into the evening in a booth at the Dew Drop Inn.

"We spent a lot of time in your father-in-law's shop, Rachelle. We also wore out a few grinding wheels on his old electric grinder making spears and arrows. We'd build up our arsenal, make a fort out of straw bales and then LeRoy, his two brothers and me would attack the fort until it looked like a porcupine. After we ran out of spears and arrows, we'd jump in the fort and pretend to fight off the attackers with our pistols and rifles. Usually a good war lasted until supper. Sometimes we'd have a running battle all over town and before we knew it, half the neighborhood was involved."

Tink looked at their faces. "I'm glad you're both here, but I know you didn't drive all the way here to just shoot the breeze. You aren't headed back to Iraq, I hope?"

"You're right, Ben." LeRoy picked up his coffee cup and swirled the remains around. "We'll be stationed in Hawaii by the time the baby comes. This may be as close as you'll get to seeing our son for awhile, unless you got a horse that can swim.

"Willy and Jim have been asking about you. They're both in Afghanistan. A lot of people have wondered if you dropped off the earth." Then he reached into his shirt pocket and pulled out a letter. "Especially Amy." Tink's face clouded.

"Now don't go flying off the handle until you hear me out. Those two fools that pulled that crap at the college and tried bringing you down with them are long gone. The Dean of your department never did want you to leave and the paper ran a full story on the deal. They backed you all the way. So did Amy. All she wants is to hear your voice."

Rachelle reached over and held Tink's hand while he stared at the unopened letter.

# NINE
## MOMMA WAS A SAILOR

Whap! The feedlot foreman's hat hit the ground, followed by a string of obscenities. *"YOU ALL GONE STUPID ON ME? PUT THE NEW BUNCH IN PEN EIGHT!"*

A balding middle-aged Coloradan, Wil had a hair-trigger temper. He threw his hat on the ground to signal that he was mad, then launched into his tirade.

Scoot reined up his horse and looked at the dusty hat lying in the alleyway. "Do you talk to your mother with that same mouth?"

Wil picked up his hat and knocked off the dirt. "She was a sailor. What's your point?"

Scoot finally got so fed up with Wil's hat tantrums that he decided on a plan to end it. He practiced throwing a ball cap to the ground, trying to mimic the sound that it made. Slapping a cupped hand to his thigh was dang close.

It wasn't long before he could put his plan into action. Wil came storming up to the hands the next morning. Scoot waited until he yanked his hat off and had just started into his windup when Scoot made the sound.

The foreman froze, staring at the ground. Hat still in hand, he began looking for it all around his feet. He even reached up with his other hand and felt his head. "What just happened here?"

Everybody but Scoot seemed just as confused as Wil. "I think you're looking for your bonnet," Scoot replied. "Maybe it's in the truck."

One of the Bucks wordlessly started to raise his arm to point at Wil's hand when the foreman spun in a 360-degree circle to make sure he hadn't missed something. He walked slowly towards the truck, placed the cap back on his head and looked at both hands like they were playing a joke on him. Everyone watched him tear his pickup apart before returning.

His eyes bounced back and forth as he took mental inventory of all the places he could have left it.

"I see you found it," Scoot said.

Wil looked like he had just been hit by lightning when Scoot pointed to his skull. The foreman reached up and pulled the hat off. He was still staring at it when everyone rode out to work the pens and feed livestock. He hadn't moved from the spot when they returned.

Tink rode up next him, leaned forward and rested his arms on the saddle horn.

"You okay, Wil?"

"Have I yelled at you boys yet?" Wil asked.

"Nah," Buck T. replied. "Your hat turned up missin', even though it was sittin' on your head big as life."

Bronc strode across the yard toward the group. "Did I tell ya'll about the time I brought a thousand head of cattle in by myself?"

"Did I tell you about the time I strangled a big mouthed ranch manager and hid his body under the wood crapper?" Wil asked. Bronc froze in his tracks.

"You stuck 'im under the outhouse? I wanna hear that one!" Buck H. climbed off his horse and looked for a seat.

Wil gave him a withering look. "I need a drink," he barked over his shoulder as he headed for the house.

"Wonder what's eatin' him?" Scoot asked.

- - # - -

*Howdy, Journal*

*Got Wil's goat today! Hope he ain't on a permanent grouch. Most everybody figured out what I'd done and gives me a nod and wink. Wil's still scratching his head, but he is keepin' a closer eye on his bonnets.*

G. L. Rasmussen

# TEN
## SEEMS LIKE A GOOD DAY TO PLAY HOOKY

Scoot's love of practical jokes came from his grandfather. Hidden beneath the handlebar mustache and permanent scowl of Charles "Chappie" Horst was a prankster of epic proportions. His weren't the whoopie cushion, plastic barf or rolling outhouses down the hill kind. They were major tactical planning and army precision pranks.

"All right, boys, we're gonna move the Carbuncle School house. I'd prefer to do it when it's occupied but we probably oughtta do it in the dark."

The Horst gang stockpiled fence poles near the white frame building by the bell. He had done it so slowly that the townsfolk really hadn't taken much notice. When everything was in place, he announced to Grandma Horst that he was going to feed the cattle and then move the Carbuncle School to a new location. Grandma just grunted and went back to sleep.

Around 4:30 a.m., he met his cohorts at the pile of poles near the school and quietly hitched a six-up team of horses to the one-room stucture. They began laying pine poles under it, drug the building to the opposite end of town and parked it on a vacant lot. A sign was hung over the door, "Cedar Pete's Saddle Repair Shop. Opening Soon." They erased their tracks and left town.

That morning, a student walked up to the group of his classmates standing silently. "Why's everybody in this empty field?"

"We think the school used to be here. See the chalk dust outline?"

"Hmmm. The bell and outhouse sure look familiar. Where's Miss Loftus? She'd know."

"She came a little bit ago, looked around and went skipping down the road singing to herself."

"This is probably as good a day as any to play hooky."

Of course, a prank of this magnitude had repercussions. It might have even been a hanging offense in those days.

The sheriff stomped around his office. "I don't allow this kind of tom foolery. Not in my town."

" Some folks reported seeing a house being towed by a team of horses a few hours ago," his deputy said.

"Did it look like the old school building?"

"They couldn't tell, Sheriff. It was too dark."

"Dang. Well, let's go to the diner and get some coffee."

Carbuncle students got an early summer break and the Gazette ran two articles and an editorial. Three weeks later, Grandpa and his gang towed the building back to its original location.

"Sheriff captures gang using school building as mobile hideout. School is back in session!" the headline read under a photo of the proud lawman. He got elected to a third term.

Sheriff Hyde spent the rest of his life trying to solve the mystery of the disappearance of "Cedar Pete's Saddle Repair Shop. Opening Soon."

G. L. Rasmussen

# ELEVEN
## DANG YOUR HIDE, I'M TRYIN' TO HELP

A wheezing cough came from the bull's pen while Scoot was making his rounds. The herd of twenty-three Longhorn and Angus crosses was being held at the feedlot for several buyers. All of them were one or two-year-olds. A bull will usually respect a horse and rider, except when they're off their feed and on the prod. Scoot suspected the wheezer would be cranky.

He opened and closed the gate a'horseback and rode into a corral brimming with horns. Fizz squeezed between the rails to follow. Scoot noticed the bull's attention shift from him to the dog. So did Fizz. *You're on your own, Boss. I just remembered I haven't, uhmm, licked myself today.* He quickly squeezed back through the gate when the herd walked his direction, leaving a sickly yearling alone in the middle of the pen.

With head down and mucus all over its muzzle, the bull looked as miserable as it sounded. Scoot had to get some shots into it fast, but when he tried to push it toward the gate, the fight began. "Dang your black hide, I'm tryin' to help!"

Then it charged. Scoot spun the buckskin just before its flank was grazed by a horn. He yelled for Tink to open the gate and run the rest of the herd down the alley.

Once the pen had emptied, except for the sick one, Scoot unlatched his rope and flipped out a loop. "Fizz!" he shouted. The dog crossed the corral in a few quick strides and sunk his teeth into an ankle. When the bull turned on Fizz, the cowboy tossed a loop around both hind legs, pulled out the slack and dallied. The buckskin backed and held her ground while Tink dropped a loop around both horns and stretched the troublemaker out.

Stepping off his horse, Scoot walked up to the bull and patted it on the back. "You ain't such an outlaw now, are ya?'"

Tink smiled. "You're lucky you got a friend on this end of the rope. I could be tempted to turn him loose and see how fast you are on your feet."

With the sick animal doctored, Tink, Wil's two boys and Scoot began sorting both of the 300 to 500 pound pens so they were uniform in weight and height and the heifers were separated from the steers.

Sorting is akin to getting grade schoolers into the right classroom on the first day. There's much confusion, noise and tears. The only one that enjoyed sorting was Fizz, mainly because he liked to hide under the fence until a calf got close, then shoot out of his hiding place, nip an ankle and watch in bemusement as the startled calf ran for its life.

Wil called the sorters together for their briefing. As he waited for the crew to assemble, he checked his new hat. It had the local feed dealer's logo on it. He had burned the "possessed" one.

"Boys, the sorting works best if it's done like this. We run about 20 to 25 head down to the end of the alley, where Tink will hold them, and decide which pen they go into. Any questions so far?

"Then each of you will work one of the three gates with the dinks, or small calves going in pen one. Second pen is for heifers, and the third for steers. Any bull calves will be run into the alley just past gate three.

"When we're done, the dinks will be run into the dink pen, bulls corralled next to the squeeze chute for denutting, then we'll sort heifers and steers according to size." The sorting went well in spite of a few miscues and Wil getting steamrolled by one of the bull calves.

The crew skipped lunch and finished castrating bull calves by suppertime. Scoot had began closing gates when a heifer changed course, ran past and decided to kick him for good measure. His thigh swelled almost instantly.

"That's gonna make life interesting for a while," he muttered to himself.

Wil and Scoot compared war wounds and decided supper and a hot bath couldn't hurt.

G. L. Rasmussen

- - # - -

*Howdy, Journal: Thursday, June 27*
*'Bout got skewered by a yearling bull. Penned*
*him up by hisself so's I can get some more shots into him.*
*Then I got kicked too near the family jewels by a little*
*heifer. The spot puffed up like a football. That's gonna*
*make climbing on and off my horse a mite touchy for a*
*bit. Had pot roast with all the fixin's tonight. I think most*
*everyone's in love with that gal. "The way to a man's*
*heart is through his stomach," Grandma used to say.*

# TWELVE
## THE RAT BALLET

Fizz turned three at the Sprocket ranch. His mother, Biscuit, had been with Scoot since he left home. Fizz came from her last litter.

Ruby fed him a piece of roast and rubbed his neck. "Where did he get his name?"

"Yeah, I been meaning to ask you that," Cody said. "I've heard 'bout every crazy name there is, but Fizz beats 'em all, hands down."

The dog turned when he heard his name, probably figuring there were more leftovers.

"He was the only black and white in the bunch. The rest were blue merles and the first ones to go when I put 'em up for sale." Scoot finished his drink in one big swallow and considered the dog lying at his feet. "He was a puff ball that reminded me of a panda, so Panda it was. Then I noticed that every time I popped the top on a can, he'd bark until I took a drink. Panda became Fizz."

59

Cody looked skeptical. "So you're tellin' me if I was to open this 'Bud', he'd start barkin'?"

"Yup. I'd rather you didn't open beer around 'im though. He's a recovering alcoholic." Cody noticed Scoot's half smile and opened his drink anyway. Fizz barked until Cody took a sip. "Don't that beat all!"

Fizz cocked his head at the can. *I don't like cats or cans hissing at me.* He barked one more time for good measure.

Scoot walked from the cook shack toward the ranch shop to finish his welding. Fizz trotted ahead. A rat ran out of the shop toward Scoot with Fizz close behind. It tried a fake left, run right. Scoot mirrored the critter's moves and was about to send a furry soul to rat heaven when it ran up his pant leg.

The "hoedown" began. Scoot danced the Texas Two-Step and the Can-Can, trying to keep the rat from getting to his nether region. Fizz barked up the pant leg, dodging flying boots. It all ended as quickly as it had begun when the rat vanished in the dust with Fizz right behind.

Scoot had undone his belt and pants and was inventorying body parts when he heard clapping and cheering. Most everybody had witnessed the performance.

He bowed. "There will be additional shows at four, six and ten."

Scoot turned to go just as Fizz dropped a dead rat

at his feet. "Good dog, but next time, kill it 'fore it goes up the pant leg. Now go brush your teeth."

Fizz sniffed the rat then looked in the direction of his owner. *"Hey boss, you forgot your lunch.* He picked up the rat and followed Scoot to the shop.

- - # - -

*Howdy, Journal: It's Saturday (I think)*

*Dang dog ran a rat up my pant leg. I didn't figure there was room, but the thing made it. Fizz killed it and then packed it around 'til I buried it. He'll probably dig it up when I ain't lookin'. Rest of the day was average.*

G. L. Rasmussen

# THIRTEEN
## I'M GONNA KICK HIS . . .

T.F. lay on his side in the parking lot of the grocery store, watching the growing ring of feet around him. *Some days it ain't worth gettin' outta bed!* he thought.

"What are you doing down there?" He recognized his wife's voice.

"Takin' a nap, what do ya think?"

Feet in violet and white shoes with sparkly laces ran and pushed their way through the crowd.

T.F. scowled. *If some guy's wearin' those, I'm gonna kick his . . . .*

"Did anyone see what happened?" The sparkly laces had a female voice.

T.F. hoped that no one had seen him get bucked off the shopping cart, but it lay next to him as evidence.

"Yeh, the old dude was cart surfing and caught a nasty wave. He's lucky there ain't no asphalt sharks."

*That's probably some pimply-faced kid,* T.F. thought. *I'm gonna kick his . . .*

The ring of feet started laughing until Mrs. Sprocket stood up. T.F. knew from experience what look she was giving them. Everyone but Sparkly Laces left.

Hands began at the back of his head and slowly worked down his spine. "Sir, I'm a doctor. Tell me if any of this hurts." He quickly inhaled when the hands touched the middle of his rib cage. "Possible broken ribs. Can you move your feet, sir? Good!"

A woman's face appeared in T.F.'s field of vision. "You're too young to be a doctor," he said. "Why don't ya run along and find your mommy?"

She laughed and began moving his arms and hands. "Didn't break your sense of humor. Can you take a deep breath for me, please? That's what I thought. You may have a punctured lung. I'm calling an ambulance."

T.F. complained to anyone who would listen while the EMT's secured the neck brace, strapped him to the gurney and loaded him into the ambulance before it drove away. Then he noticed his wife following. *I'll never hear the end a'this!*

"That woman's a hit man. Shouldn't somebody be calling the police?" he groused.

The EMT's glanced out the window, then at each other and put an oxygen mask on their patient.

T.F. was terrorizing the ER staff when Doc Hornsby, the family doctor, finally showed up and had the nurse give him a dose of Demerol. From then on, he was a kitten. The doctor had considered keeping T.F.

overnight until the staff all threatened to quit. Hornsby sent him home.

The ranch kept on running while he was recuperating, which seemed to vex him. So, just to keep things in kelter, he'd sit on his front porch and fire everybody from there. His wife finally just left him outside with a sandwich and a bucket to pee in.

"You can come inside when you behave yourself," she ordered.

He eventually toned it down, at least until he'd healed enough to get out of the chair by himself. "Shopping cart" got erased from the ranch lexicon.

- - # - -

*Howdy, Journal: June 29*

*T.F. and the Mrs. came back from a day of shopping for the ranch. T.F. was all banged up. He won't say how, and we ain't gonna ask. If he's a firecracker on good days, he's gonna be a volcano for a while!*

G. L. Rasmussen

# FOURTEEN
## THE ACORN DIDN'T FALL FAR

Summer was one of the hotter ones in memory. T.F. remained his irascible self, although he did add some chairs to his front porch when it became the gathering place after suppertime. He seemed to enjoy the attention, even though he made a halfhearted effort to run people off.

Complaints aside, rancher Sprocket spoke fondly of his cowboying days, something he enjoyed more than the day-to-day duties of owning a ranch. He even told the bunch on his porch about the time he bought an airplane from some big city dude who landed right on the dirt road leading to the place.

"'All the big ranches have planes,' says the dude. 'You'll save so much time you can take your wife out to dinner every week.' The salesman stopped in the middle of his pitch when he noticed I wasn't smiling. 'Okay, you'll save so much time that you can throw back a few beers with your buddies and play some cards.' Nothing.

'Uhmmm, get back in the saddle?'

"That was the clincher," T.F. said. "I took a few flying lessons, didn't bother to take the final test and buzzed Sprocket Land and Livestock in my Cessna. Then the Feds told me I had to get my license or park it. What're ya gonna do, shoot me down? I asked. Pencil necked sonsab . . . Then one of them guys pretended he had an anti-aircraft gun and was strafing the Red Baron. My plane went down the road after I thought about it for a bit.

"I ain't gonna play the guv'mint's games. Hell, my parents never had a license for anything, except to get married. They bought their first car in '31 from ol' Bent Kinsett. Haven't thought of him for awhile. He's been dead about thirty years, now.

"Anyway, the two oldest boys and Pa got the hang of driving, but Ma never did. Pa thought she wasn't doing too badly until she ran the car through the back of the garage and on through the blacksmith shop. The Chevy finally came to roost in the chicken coop." T.F. laughed and slapped his leg.

"Pa came a' runnin' outta the house yellin', 'Who's making that racket?' Us kids pointed at our feather-covered mother. 'Wha . . . What's with all the dead chickens?' he asked.

Our Mom didn't have much patience. 'They're for supper, what did you think they're for?'

'Six of 'em?'

"She pushed Pop out of the way and flung open the door, scattering feathers into the house. 'That's how many I killed, OK?'

"'Did you use a machine gun? Ha, ha, ha.'

"'No, the car,' she said.

"Pa got serious real quick. 'You ran over them?'

"Then Mom's voice got all funny like she was tellin' a good joke. 'Only two of them. A flying anvil hit one; the other three were killed when the hen house roof collapsed. Now go fix the coop and round up the survivors. I'll make supper.'"

T.F. was gasping for breath and pounding the arm of his chair. "Those two were a kick in the pants."

- - # - -

*Howdy, Journal: Hot as hell, probably July.*

*The Boss was in a good mood today, most likely the pain pills. Told us about his folks. The acorn didn't fall far from the tree. Seems like he's mostly healed from "the wreck." He's a tough old bird. Don't know how or why his wife puts up with him.*

G. L. Rasmussen

# FIFTEEN
## THE DYNAMIC DUO

The wind picked up and lightning flashes lit the distant hills to the west. A storm was coming Scoot's way, so he hurried to get the siphon tubes laid out and irrigation water started on hayfield number one. The flashes came with such frequency that it resembled a strobe.

In a matter of minutes, the storm front had cleared the nearest hill and dropped a bolt in his vicinity, just to let him know it had arrived. Scoot blinked his eyes trying to get them adjusted back to the darkness when something shot between his legs at a dead run. It resembled Fizz with a 'fro. *Move it, the microwave exploded!*

"What's next?" Scoot groused.

A downpour answered. He figured he had one of three choices to make:

1. Stand there and drown.

2. Get turned into a charcoal briquette by a lightning bolt.

3. Be eaten by a marauding pack of wolves.

Number 3 was probably the least likely but it's nice to have several choices. He finally decided that changing the irrigation set, hoping that Mother Nature was a poor shot and then running for the truck seemed the best idea. Another flash nearby made the decision for him. Scoot finished moving and starting the siphon tubes in record time and sprinted up the hill.

Fizz waited under the truck, dry, smiling and ready to go. *Next time you decide to play in the rain, leave the keys.*

Scoot thought about leaving him for the wolves.

Driving away, he could see the storm spreading across the valley. He reached the cook shack just in time for supper, left his rubber boots on the porch and walked through the door.

Ruby stopped in middle of dishing up a plate for one of the crew. "You're dripping wet!"

"Yup, that I am. I got caught in a rainstorm, almost electrified and nearly run down by my own dog. I think I'm going to fire Fizz. He's never around when I'm in a tight spot."

"Where was he all the time you were getting soaked to the skin?"

"Uhmmm, under the truck staying dry," he stammered.

"So who's the smart one in that dynamic duo?" she purred.

Scoot decided not to reply. Some questions don't deserve a response.

72

- - # - -

*Howdy, Journal: July 2*
*Dang dog! Fizz runs away from a little bolt of lightening and a gully-washer of a rainstorm and hides under the truck. 'Course, he ain't good at startin' siphon tubes and don't have the first clue about moving a dam.*
*Probably oughtta quit whining and change into some dry clothes.*

G. L. Rasmussen

## SIXTEEN
### MOSES WAS A COWBOY

Tink flung open the screen door on Scoot's place then jumped out of the way before it slammed shut. "That coyote trap you call a door's gonna take somebody's leg off. Hey, there's a cowboy church commencin' at ten in Newton, then they strap a feed bag on us afterwards. You in?"

Scoot closed his sketchbook and slid it in the bookcase. "Sure, as long as the feedin' part lasts longer than the preaching part."

"Don't know about that, but at least we get off the spread for a bit."

"Yeh, I'm in."

Cowboy church goers appreciated the casual attire and Pastor Boots Fehnder's "cowboyfied" Bible teachings. Boots got the call to preach while in a coma from a truck wreck. His dead grandpa came to him in a dream and ordered Boots to spread God's word and become a golf pro.

Since Boots had never golfed, grandpa must have got that part wrong. Now he could devote even more time to spreading the word.

Boots formed a choir from retired and working waitresses, unless they had the breakfast shift, and the piano player came from the Dew Drop Inn, which gave the music a decidedly honky tonk flavor. A portable chalkboard announced the sermon: "Moses leads the children of Israel."

Pastor Boots attempted to get the crowd's attention when a hulk of a cowboy stood and looked around. The room went quiet.

"Thanks, Grizz. Ladies and Gents, let's visit a bit about Moses. He's kinda like the ranch owner's son only he ain't really kin 'cause the owner's daughter found him as a baby floatin' down the creek behind the homestead."

A hand went up at the back of the room. "Was he dead?"

"Was who dead, Mike?"

"Moses. Why's he floatin' in the crick?"

"He's fly fishin', genius. You never heard about his mom makin' him a boat and puttin' them in the crick?" Mike's neighbor asked.

Mike looked stunned. "My momma was one fine mechanic but she never built me no boat!"

The crowd went silent.

"Thanks, Grizz. Moses had been put in a boat made from reeds 'cause his mother couldn't keep him, but that's a whole 'nother story. Anyway, he got raised in high cotton and had it dang good. Moses got the best horses, food, clothes, everything. Then he whooped the daylights out of the ranch foreman who was whippin' on Moses' friend and got run off the place.

"Well, here's ol' Moses walking through the desert when God starts talking to him out of this burnin' bush and He says, "I want you to go back there and git the rest of the crew. I got a better spread for ya'll to work at."

Moses wasn't too sure about doing that because he ain't so good at speakin', but he figures having God on his side is just like team roping with a guy that never misses. So Moses does just that and before you know it, him and the rest of the hands are walking out through the desert. Then they commence to complaining 'cause it's lunchtime and there ain't no feed wagon acomin'.

"Well, Moses talks to God a'gin and God says not to worry about the food, He's got it covered. Then they look around and there's 'manna' layin' everywhere." Several hands went up. "Manna is God's version of steak and eggs." The hands went down.

"Then the boys were gettin' a mite parched so Moses hits a rock with this stick and water comes out."

Several hands were raised. "Hey, Boots, was there any beer rocks?"

"Naw, they didn't have no beer rocks."

"How about coffee rocks? There's gotta be coffee rocks, don't there?"

"Nope. There wasn't any beer rocks, coffee rocks, lemonade rocks or whiskey rocks." Hands started dropping until one remained. Jeff Parkins.

"Is God a Mormon, Boots?"

"Not sure on that one, Jeff."

"Maybe Moses just lived in a dry county or somethin'." Laughter erupted then quit.

"Thanks, Grizz. Where was I?"

"God was dishing up grub and Moses kept wackin' rocks."

"Oh, yeh. Thanks again, Grizz. Well, things are goin' pretty good until they sees that the rancher is riding down on them with a bunch of new hands and they're intendin' to get even with Moses and the boys.

So God and Moses part the river so's him and his boys can walk across on dry land. Which is good since all of them had on their good boots. Then the river closed up on that ol' rancher and his boys. After that, all's ya see is hats floatin' away.

"One day the Lord had Moses come to the top of a mountain and gives him the Ten Commandments that said it was against God's laws to steal your neighbor's water or covet his good rope horse or shoot him for no good reason. Plus we're 'sposed to love God, our folks and the neighbors, not go to the saloon on Sundays and things like that.

"Soon Moses and the cowboys learned that when they did that stuff, things went better and life ain't so haywired. Now, how about a song from the Newton Waitresses and Retired Bar Maids' Choir."

Scoot and Tink put away several plates of darn good barbeque, potato salad and homemade root beer.

They even did some socializing. The two decided this church thing might not be half bad.

- - # - -

*Howdy, Journal: Sunday*
        *Got preached to and then fed. Boots had an interesting take on the story of Moses, and a choir complete with piano. They weren't too bad. Probably be better if they all used the same notes. Ruby couldn't come with us.*

G. L. Rasmussen

## SEVENTEEN
### NEWTON PUTS ON BELLS

Newton was a sleepy, out-of-the-way place. If a person didn't live there, he had to be real lost to find it. When the Fourth of July rolled around, the town woke up and put bells on. Flags hung everywhere. The cannon guarding the entrance to the main square got a good cleaning by the local Boy and Girl Scout troop and the rodeo stands had another coat of paint slapped on.

Mayor Dunford started wearing one of those flat-topped straw hats and a red, white and blue bowtie a month before the celebration. Military uniforms were resurrected from mothballs; horses and tack, trucks, tractors, even prize bulls were cleaned and polished for Newton's Independence Day Extravaganza Parade.

The town got barricaded off for the parade. Even a few hapless travelers joined the town folk and neighboring farmers and ranchers.

It wasn't long before even captured spectators got into the spirit of the occasion and ended up staying for the noon feed. Some stayed longer once they started sampling the home brew.

Entries for the parade had to be secured a year in advance, except for Dusty Draper who rode his trained longhorn steer in the lead. The Granddaughters of the Early Settlers Club's float came next, followed by the fire department throwing candy from the back of the old pumper truck.

One of the longstanding entries in the Newton parade was the Sprocket Ranch chuck wagon, which was then parked in the town square next to the city fathers' two half-beeves on a spit. Pies, salads, desserts and taters in every imaginable form began appearing on the rows of tables.

Ruby volunteered to bake several Dutch oven cobblers and Fizz volunteered to sit in the shade under the wagon and wait for some kid to lay down his plate. *I believe a dog needs priorities. "Food" is my top three.*

The newly founded Newton Waitress and Retired Barmaid Choir sang the National Anthem at the flag raising ceremony. Ranchers' Association put on a carnival, which included apple bobbing, a dunk tank, roping dummies, miniature Ferris wheel, dart and balloon toss, knock-down-the-milk-bottles and guess-where-the-chicken-will-poop raffle. Several hat, saddle, bit and spur makers, plus the local used car dealer, had booths.

Across the square and separate from everyone sat the fifty-something hippie chick and her Earth Mother Crafts booth.

Fireworks were never a part of the entertainment because of the tinder dry conditions, so the celebration usually ended with banjo and fiddle music, a dance and the sheriff breaking up several fights.

One fight broke out over the chicken poop raffle because no one kept watch and the chicken had pooped three times. Now that there were multiple winners, the mayor had to be called in to judge the age of the three droppings. He suggested that the county coroner do it, but the coroner had already judged the home brew and then passed out under the town's historic elm tree.

A winner was chosen after three coin tosses. Grizz Potts proudly displayed his new handmade quilt. The two losers decided that the chicken had cheated and were going the shoot it until a blonde ten year-old rescued Miss Cluck, her pet. Festivities broke up around 1 a.m.

The turkey shoot, a new addition to the festivities, followed the Newton Rodeo that Saturday.

Bucking stock came from rodeo contractor, Twist Jenkins, who even did the announcing a'horseback. He used the same jokes every year but they still busted the crowds up. Why change good material? The clowns were a couple locals boys and the pickup men were Twist's two sons. Contestants came from all around the county.

The rodeo didn't attract outsiders mostly because there wasn't any money in it, just bragging rights. Toad Beldon outrode everybody in the bulls and bareback broncs, and even took a second in the team roping with Scoot as header. 'Course, Toad was on the rodeo team at

UNLV and could ride the hide off about anything before he began walking.

The rodeo ended on a high note. No one got killed and except for a couple broken bones, the EMT's really had nothing to do but down a few beers and keep out of the sun and sight of the town's divorcees. The following Monday, Newton's Fourth of July Committee deemed this year's festivities a success and started to work on the next one. First order of business: the name of the celebration. Newton's First Annual Rodeo and Turkey Shoot became Newton F.A.R.T.S. Not exactly how an upstanding community wanted its biggest celebration of the year to be known.

- - # - -

*July 4th*

*Had a nice day at Newton's Fourth. A lot of good people in these parts. Team roped with some of the boys from the ranch, got second place riding with Toad Beldon. What a hand!*

*Fizz hung out with Ruby, unless there were easier pickins' somewhere else. It's a good thing he has a job or he'd be fat as a tick all the time. Tink has been quieter than usual. Says he's just thinkin'. Hope he ain't thinkin' of leaving.*

# EIGHTEEN
## SCOOT AND BONEHEAD

When the ranch discovered that Scoot had a way with horses, especially the young, difficult ones, he found himself up to his eyeballs in unbroken colts. Horses communicate with one another through body language and Scoot was fluent in that language. Even T.F. loitered at a respectful distance to watch Scoots' magical touch at work. T.F. had seen the transition from the once brutal breaking practices to the evolution of horse psychology, a trainer's ability to connect with a horse on more than just a physical level.

The ability to read the animal's moods, movements and thought processes had changed the equine world forever. Also, through selective breeding, choosing the right sire and dam to enhance natural athleticism and intelligence, generations of horse "super stars" were being born.

Scoot had been working with a particularly frustrating colt that he named "Bonehead." They weren't connecting and that's when Scoot committed a cardinal

85

sin. He entered the arena that day with the intention of forcing his own agenda on a horse that had other plans.

After brushing and saddling, they moved down the alleyway towards a pen full of five-hundred-pound calves, or five weights, that hadn't been processed yet. The horse pulled back on the reins a bit as the calves scattered when he and Scoot approached the gate.

Once inside the pen, Scoot mounted up and started working the colt quietly in a small circle, asking him to flex his body and move off leg pressure. He noticed how the horse kept his ears and eyes on the herd and was reluctant to turn his backside to them. Then they approached a few stragglers that were hanging back from the main body of the group and applied a little pressure to move them. Bonehead would drop his head whenever he got near one of the calves and sniff at it, a good sign.

It was while they were playing a little game of tag that they got too close to the rest of the herd and broke the bubble, putting too much pressure on the outside edge of the main bunch. Pandemonium broke out.

Calves ran and crashed into the corner gate, knocking it over. The colt reared, slipping in the wet footing and came down on its right side and Scoot's leg. Scoot managed to kick his feet out of the stirrups but couldn't get that leg clear of the horse. His left foot got hung up in the back cinch and his head hit a fence rail.

Before losing consciousness, he tipped the horse's nose up and dallied the outside rein around the saddle horn so it couldn't get up and drag him. Then everything went black.

# NINETEEN
## YOU'RE GONNA BE THE DEATH OF ME

Ruby slid a pan of buttermilk biscuits in the oven. Her hair was bunched under an old bandana and she had her trademark flour on the tip of her nose. She straightened with a jolt. Something didn't feel right. Ruby scanned the kitchen then looked out the window. Calves were in the yard. They shouldn't have been, at least not without a cowboy horseback and moving them somewhere. Then the thought crossed her mind: *Scoot's in trouble!* She shut off the oven, crashed through the door and front gate, scattering cattle as she ran towards the pens.

At first she couldn't see anything until she heard a horse's stressed snort and spotted it lying on its side with its nose in the air. Tink and one of the Bucks were coming up the lane. She screamed at them and then sprinted towards the corral. She instinctively knew not to run at the horse.

Walking slowly and talking quietly, she wrapped the horse's head in her arms and cradled it while stroking the muzzle. Ruby could see Scoot and he wasn't moving. The two cowboys followed her lead and walked carefully to the horse's side. They checked each leg for breaks and blood.

Tink stepped to Scoot's side. "Keep the horse's head tipped up, Ruby, 'til we get Scoot unraveled."

More riders pulled into the yard. Buck waved Matt Clegg over.

"Come up careful on your horse and give me your rope." When Buck had the loop around Scoot's saddle horn, he had Matt dally. "Okay, Ruby, keep aholt of the reins and when I say 'Now', you pull while Matt helps the colt up and me and Tink will push it away from Scoot. Okay, NOW!"

Bonehead rolled onto his folded legs, gave a grunt then stood up. Another of the hands took the reins when Ruby lunged and slid over to Scoot on her knees. She gently stroked his face while Tink put his ear to the unconscious cowboy's chest to listen for a heartbeat. Suddenly Scoot took a deep breath, moaned and slowly opened his eyes. "Dang," he whispered, "Heaven smells like cow-doo, but at least the angels look like Ruby."

She picked up his hat, reshaped it and sat next to the injured cowboy.

"You're gonna be the death of me." Reaching for his hand, she squeezed it. "You ever considered a safer occupation?"

"I've always wanted to be a dynamite tester."

Ruby swatted him with his own hat.

The EMTs' gave him a good going over, put him on a gurney and placed it into the ambulance. "You've got quite a knot on that head, probably a concussion. That right knee is out of the socket and there are at least a couple bruised ribs, maybe even broken. You need some x-rays, Scoot, and probably a couple days in the hospital just to be safe."

"Nah, I'm all right," Scoot said, "I'll just lay off for a bit."

"Oh no, you're not, cowboy," Ruby broke in. "You're going if I have to drag you." Then she put her face down close to his and whispered, "Please."

Scoot smiled. "It doesn't pay to lock horns with you, does it?"

Fizz sat and watched the ambulance slowly climb the small rise after one of the EMT's stopped him from jumping in the rear door. Scoot simply said, "Stay!"

Ruby visited with Fizz and gave him a hug before she got back in the ambulance. The sad and confused-looking dog didn't move until the rest of the crew turned and walked toward the houses. Buck looked over his shoulder and nodded for Fizz to come with them. "You can bunk with me until your pard gets back. It'll only be a couple days."

Fizz sat and considered his options. *Okay, but I get the bed and I don't do Dog Chow.* He trotted after the cowboys.

The two days in the hospital flew by. Ruby was there when Scoot went to sleep and when he woke. They were able to talk almost nonstop. She also ran off the nurses that came in the wee hours to check his vitals.

The cowboy enjoyed being mother-henned by Ruby as much as she did doing it, even though he grew weary of the hospital food and the air-conditioned gown. The dream about him riding the feedlot pens in a hospital gown was very troubling, although Ruby got a kick out of the story. She bought one of them and hid it amongst Scoot's belongings.

He sorely missed his sketchbooks, but most of all, he needed to get back to the spread and make things right with Bonehead.

And Fizz.

- - # - -

The Paint colt watched Scoot limp up to the pen and lean on the gate. When the cowboy began speaking softly, the two-year-old walked over. Scoot stroked his forehead and Bonehead pressed his face to Scoot's chest to be rubbed behind the ears and all over his muzzle. Scoot decided the horse deserved a new name. Zip came to mind.

*I might as well keep the "Z" thing going.*

Then he checked his pocket for dog treats and whistled for Fizz.

- - # - -

*Howdy, Journal: July10*

*Home at last! I'm free of that antiseptic smellin', noisy-as-a-kindergarten-bus hospital. I will miss having Ruby's undivided attention though.*

*My roommate was an older gent. I think he's on the downward slide 'cos he kept repeating himself. The nurses were always asking him if he needed to use the bathroom. "Why do I have to go in there? I gotta diaper on." He constantly asked my name while we were getting ready to leave. Thought Ruby was his daughter.*

G. L. Rasmussen

# TWENTY
## A MAN OF MEANS

When two worlds slip into the same orbit and collide like Ruby and Scoot, the whole universe gets knocked off kelter.

Scoot was pushing thirty and had been enjoying the single, unencumbered life. He bounced from job to job and never had trouble finding work, but the thoughts of putting down roots had become foreign to him. Now, the idea of settling down was a bit of a relief, since as a child he had only known one home and even though he liked the idea of just kicking around, it had grown old.

Once he accepted the inevitable, Scoot had to turn his mind to the thought of creating a future for Ruby and him. Of course, he had skipped a few important steps on the way to their bliss: he hadn't asked Ruby to marry him, and even before that, he needed to run the idea past Ruby's grandparents, who had raised her since she was twelve. But first, he phoned his parents.

"Merritt's."

93

"Hi, Mom."

"Scoot? Is that you? You finally figured out how to use a telephone?"

"Has it been that long?"

"Ya think? Dad, it's Scoot."

"Who?"

"Scoot, our son."

"What? He finally figured out how to use the telephone?"

"Okay, Mom, you made your point."

"So what's the occasion? You're not dying are you?"

"Mom!"

"I'm sorry, honey, it's wonderful to hear from you . . . but you aren't dying, right?"

"No I'm not. I am thinking of gettin' hitched though - - Hello?"

"I thought this was Scoot. You're an insurance salesman, aren't you?"

"I'm trying to be serious here!"

"Okay, dear, I'll be serious, too. This isn't about Amway either, right?"

"Okay, Mom, I'll just send you an invitation . . . if she'll have me. See ya."

"Whoa there cowboy, you are serious! This is exciting. Now tell me all about her.   Wait a minute . . . *Dad, Scoot's getting married.*"

"Uh-huh. This is about Amway, isn't it? They'll say anything to get their foot in the door."

"*Get serious, Hugh!* All right, tell me everything about her."

"Well, she's got long reddish hair, green eyes that look right through me and a smile that can melt ya. She knows me but still likes me.

"Before I met her, all I needed was to be sittin' on a horse. Now, I just want to be with her. I don't know, Mom, it's kinda got me spooked. First off, I can't understand what she sees in me and second, I don't have anything to offer her except me for the rest of our lives - - Hello?"

"(Sniff) You really love this gal, don't you? Well, first off, any girl would be lucky to have you. Secondly, you're not exactly a man without means. *Hugh, come and tell your boy about that land he owns*."

"Is it time? Okay, I'm coming. Son, we haven't said anything before now because you've been jumping around like a fart in a frying pan, but Grandma left you that section of ground with the old homestead on it.

"The house could use some fixing but it's sound. Grandpa has been leasing the ground and putting the rent payments into an account for you. You're worth a tidy little sum. Congratulations, Scoot . . . Scoot? Great, I think I killed him."

"Scoot?"

"Thanks, Mom. I need some time to process all of this. Besides, there's a couple other folks that should probably hear all this. And one of them is Ruby. I love you two."

That last part made Mother Merritt so giddy that after she hung up, she danced around the room and then waltzed into the living room, sat on Hugh's lap and hugged him. He figured she'd gone over the edge.

# TWENTY-ONE
## WHERE'S MY PARD'?

An especially dry and lightning-loaded front passed through one day and peppered the distant hills.

Soon smoke billowed from a couple of different spots on T-Bar-S's range and the phone rang a short time later at Sprocket's. Ruby filled the coolers and the hands loaded the D-9 bulldozer and picks and shovels. They could wait in vain for the government smoke jumpers or get pre-emptive.

Range fires were the cost of doing business and if one leased government land for grazing, you lived with the fact that the government's hands-off policies just made their land the breeding ground for giant infernos.

The T-Bar-S hands were already at work and backed up by the crew from the Three Peaks Ranch. Other help would be arriving soon. Everyone knew the drill, and except for a few cowboys that were a'horseback trying to move cattle out of harm's way, the rest were working on firebreaks.

A second dozer churned up dust near the top of a small rise where it had cut two miles of break. The Sprocket D-9 Caterpillar headed perpendicular on a southeast path from the new cut just in case the wind shifted and pushed the fire in a different direction.

While Scoot and the crew worked to clear brush around a line shack and some loafing pens, two cowboys ran about 30 head of cattle past them, then dropped out of sight over a hill down towards the meadows and Stoney Creek. Hopefully the cows would put the creek and green grass between them and any approaching flames.

Smoke was still visible in the distance but flames weren't. Two more loaded bulldozers could be seen on the main access road a mile and a half away from the Sprocket bunch. It looked like they were trying to get ahead of the first crew and clear more brush. If T.F.'s crew could cut a break to the canyon where Stoney Creek dropped off in a hundred-foot waterfall, the width of the gorge would hold the fire.

Townsfolk showed up just before dark, some to offer help, others to rubberneck. Smoke jumpers finally pulled in after that. Once the wind died down, late evening dew slowed the fire's progress.

The government crews worked for a week to contain the twelve-thousand acre fire. Mop-up lasted another day. When the fire crews and trucks finally pulled out, the Sprocket crew moved in.

- - # - -

Cold, wet and tired, the little dog forced himself to keep going. He had followed the stream since tumbling into it while chasing a rabbit. Fizz had never worked so hard for a meal, only to watch it effortlessly disappear over a rise. *I need to hunt slower food.*

Sage grouse broke from cover several times right in front of his face but he didn't glance at them. Then he heard a howl. *The wild dogs are coming.* Somewhere deep inside he knew that the coyote was calling others for dinner and Fizz was on the menu.

He surprised a doe and her fawn drinking from a shallow pool next to the slow moving water. The pair bolted, jumped over the sage along the creek bed and trotted up the hillside, heads high and ears pointed back toward the black and white dog.

With lungs burning and his feet bleeding, Fizz waded in the stream a ways before pushing on into the night, thinking of his master. *The boss'll be right around the next turn. He has to be.*

- - # - -

Scoot tossed two coffee cans full of oats into the feeder for his horses and started hanging up tack and saddles. The day had been hot, dusty and long. He normally brushed and washed his buckskin mare and bay gelding before putting them up, but today had worn all of them down to the point where only food and sleep could put them right.

He took one last look around. He hadn't been tripping over Fizz since they returned to the ranch. *The mutt probably went right to the cook shack to mooch off Ruby.*

The Sprocket hands had pulled away from headquarters that morning while the thermostat read a warm seventy-four degrees. By noon, the sun had pushed the seventy-four to over a hundred. Everyone - - cowboys, horses, cattle and dogs - - seemed to move in slow motion. Fizz jumped into the stock tank at every break in the work and then found a spot of shade until Scoot whistled him back on duty.

They were working with T-Bar-S hands, separating cattle to be moved to their respective home grounds. The fire had mixed herds. Those that were missing brands got one and those that had testicles and shouldn't, had them confiscated.

Most of the activity centered at the T-Bar-S pens, a mile onto their turf and nearly twenty from Sprocket headquarters. When T.F.'s cattle were separated out, they would be pushed over to their side toward Stoney Creek.

Cowboys stomped boots and swatted dust from their clothes with even dustier hats. A few groans and a "What a day!" could be heard, but most were silent. Only the smell of food kept them moving.

Matt Clegg trotted toward the group. Tink shook his head. "Geez, Matt, are you too young or too dumb to be tired?"

"Yup," Matt said, grinning. He squeezed thru the door ahead of Scoot. "Where's your sidekick?"

"Where *is* my sidekick? I figured Fizz would be first in line."

"Probably inside lickin' his chops. Ruby's partial to the little mooch." Tink slapped Scoot on the back and followed him inside.

Scoot glanced around the chow hall and had a sick feeling grab his gut. Ruby saw the look and instantly dropped the ladle onto the counter. "Scoot! Where's Fizz?"

"Anybody seen my dog since we pulled in?" Only blank stares answered.

"He rode with you, didn't he? Him and two or three other dogs jumped onto your flatbed while we were loading horses." Buck T. looked out the window. "He ain't outside, Scoot. You know he's always here when chows on."

"Oh, hell, Scoot, we saw 'im!" Buck H. pointed at Cody. "Remember that skunk we thought we saw back where Stoney went under the road? That was Fizz!"

"Dang, Buck. We shoulda stopped."

"Anybody that wants to help, let's load up! Better be packin' a weapon!" Scoot ran out the door to the corrals. Ruby followed on his heels. She didn't say a word but grabbed a halter and climbed over the top rail of the horse pen. Scoot knew that look. She was going.

- - # - -

The desert air had cooled when Fizz got his second wind. He picked up the pace, staying near the water, only stopping occasionally to check his back trail. He didn't see or hear them but knew they were coming.

The stream moved faster. Fizz heard a distant roar. He had traveled the four miles from the road where he fell off the truck to the hundred-foot drop of Stoney Creek Falls. Up the mountainside or out into the desert were the only two options left to him now. Yet he knew he couldn't outrun or outfight a pack of coyotes.

- - # - -

Five coyotes long-trotted beside the creek, slowing enough to check Fizz's trail, then move on. Fresh and hungry, they could cover twice the ground their prey could. Rounding a bend, they stopped and milled, noses to the ground. There was a cross trail. Fizz's scent disappeared, but two deer had been here, one a fawn. The leader and three others yipped and howled before turning to sprint up the hill. The chorus fell silent when one of the coyotes whined further downstream. It had found Fizz's trail.

# Twenty-two
## You Hurt My Dog

Two trucks pulling stock trailers thundered to a stop just past the culvert where Stoney Creek passes under the road and continues on toward the falls. A full moon painted glistening stars on the tumbling water and cast shadows from the horses and men in the strange ballet.

Scoot stopped tightening the cinch on the mare at the first howl. "There's a pack toward the falls." Answering howls came from further up the mountain and behind the group upstream.

"Ruby and I'll head down the creek. Tink, Buck T. and Cody go the opposite direction. Matt and Buck H. move up to the bench above Ruby and me. Fire three shoots if you find . . . uhh, anything."

They swung into their saddles, scrambled down the sides of the road and kicked their mounts into a run.

- - # - -

Fizz jumped onto a rocky shelf to consider his scanty options. The roar from the falls was distracting and the sense that the pack would be upon him soon kept him pacing. He wanted a drink from one of the many small pools just below the rocks.

Moving carefully down the stone steps, Fizz leaned toward the water when he saw movement. Five shadows weaved in and out of the bushes by the creek. The pack's noses unerringly followed his trail. Deep in his throat, a low growl rumbled and hackles rose while he backed away from the streams-edge to creep back to the rocks. Fizz had decided to try and run when a cleft in the rocks, barely bigger than him, offered some protection. He backed into it.

In moments, the coyotes were working their way toward his hiding place, weaving back and forth, searching for the freshest scent. Fizz watched the dark figures move his way. The leader, with its yellow eyes glowing from the moonlight, stared right at him. Fizz pushed back into the cleft as far as he could.
The fight was coming and he was ready.

- - # - -

Scoot and Ruby ran their horses as fast as they dared along the stream. "There's four or five coyotes sticking to a trail and it ain't a deer or rabbit. I'll watch this side and you watch the other to see if they turn off. If I jerk my rifle, grab the reins. My saddle pistol is on the offside. I'll be the tall coyote in case you start blasting."

- - # - -

All five drew closer to Fizz. They crisscrossed in front of the small opening, testing the ground and trying to draw the meal out. One made a rush at the opening. Fizz bit into the soft flesh of its muzzle and shook as it yelped, finally tearing itself free. As soon as the first pulled out of the entrance, another came in.

The second grabbed Fizz's paw just above the ankle but Fizz raked the side of its face with his canines, tearing open an eyelid and an eye. It yelped and let loose of his paw, jumped back and rubbed at the socket with a foreleg. The rest withdrew from Fizz's view. He panted and trembled, waiting for the next attack.

He began to feel trapped, vulnerable. He considered running. Then two muzzles forced themselves into the opening. One grabbed the little dog's ear, the other got a hold on his throat. He couldn't move, fight or make a noise. He couldn't breath. His body began relaxing and preparing for the inevitable. There was calmness in the midst of this death struggle. He closed his eyes.

- - # - -

Scoot sensed more than knew where Fizz was and that he was in severe trouble. Then he saw the coyotes. He slide the mare to a stop, jerked the rifle from the scabbard as he jumped off and began running. He stopped long enough to snap off a round at the two by the rocks and follow some movement going up the hillside before firing again. He sprinted up the hill to the rocks and fired again. Another coyote burst from cover, running toward the stream. Three shots in rapid succession came from behind Scoot. He glanced to see the coyote cartwheel down the incline.

Rounding the rock shelf, Scoot came upon the bodies of two coyotes. He grabbed them by the tails and dragged them aside, peering into the opening. "Fizz, are you in there, pup?"

- - # - -

The report of the rifle seemed miles and lifetimes away. Finally, the pain eased and breaths came in short, rasping gulps. Fizz lay in his fortress, eyes closed. Somewhere in the back of his head came a voice that he recognized, then two. He whimpered when hands slid him out of the crevasse.

-- # --

Scoot carefully picked the little dog up and began checking the damage where blood was visible. Ruby gently stroked his head and spoke softly to him, her voice breaking. Still clutching the saddle pistol, she looked around at the scene. The leader lay where Scoot had dragged him. Then his yellow eyes blinked, he jumped to his feet and started toward the shadows. Ruby spun around and lifted the Colt. "You hurt my dog you son-of-a-CRACK! The smell of spent gunpowder floated away and the yellow eyes emptied of life.

Horses crashed through the brush and then splashed in the creek. Tink was the first to reach the site. "Hell, you two, it sounded like a war zone. I passed a dead one lying next to Stoney."

A shot reverberated farther up the incline. "There's another one that ain't gonna give us trouble." It was Buck H.'s voice. "You hit it in the shoulder."

Buck T. led their horses across the stream. "That one down there has three holes in him. How'd you git so many shots off, Scoot?"

"Gentlemen, meet Miss Annie Oakley, or should I say, Ruby Oakley. She had my back."

Ruby hid the gun behind her and looked at the ground. "Grampa was an Army marksman in Korea. He showed me a few things."

"Is Fizz gonna make it?" Tink asked.

"I don't know, but we'd better get a move on to find out. He's tore up a might but ain't lost much blood. This dog's a thinker. He holed up instead of trying to run for it. We wouldn't have found a hair if he hadn't."

It was a race back to the trailers and the horses were hastily loaded. Ruby held the bloodied dog all the way to the vet's. Fizz's eyes opened and he appeared to be listening to Ruby's encouragement. The lack of food and stress from nearly being eaten had taken its toll.

"Fizz can't ever ride anywhere but in the truck from now on. Deal?"

Scoot had already come to that conclusion, but Ruby's pleadings touched him.

"Deal," he said.

Scoot had never been comfortable around women, but he found himself drawn to Ruby and the security of her company. The near loss of Fizz brought feelings bubbling to the surface and the constant care of the little dog offered an opportunity to be together in other ways besides fishing.

He replayed the rescue of Fizz in his head. Especially the part when Ruby shouted, "You hurt my dog!" Suddenly it felt like Ruby had always been in their lives. Scoot was okay with that notion.

- - # - -

*Howdy, Journal: It's been a tough day*

*Almost lost Fizz. I guess he fell or got knocked off the truck near Stoney Creek and roughed up by a bunch of coyotes. He held 'em off 'til we got there. The vet cleaned him up and asked that we leave him for a bit. Strange, I wrote "we."*

*I take too many things for granted and I've been thinkin' 'bout my life and everyone and everything that makes it worth livin'. The little mutt, rest of the crew and Ruby has gotten aholt of my heart. The thought that one day they may not be here twists my gut.*

G. L. Rasmussen

# TWENTY-THREE
## AIN'T WORTH A PLUG NICKLE

Ruby knew something was up. The evening meal needed serving but this was more important. Scoot had become withdrawn and quiet and she sincerely hoped it didn't have something to do with her. Not being one to brood over the unknown, Ruby flat out asked him, "Okay, Scoot, what's going on? You're starting to worry me." He stared into her eyes for what seemed an eternity.

"I've been wantin' to ask you to marry me for awhile now, but I was too embarrassed. 'I ain't worth a plug nickel' I kept tellin' myself. All I have is a useless dog that would take on a grizzly bear for you, two horses, and a truck that T.F. still owns the majority of."

Fizz sat up and looked around. *Grizzlies? Can't be worse than that bunch of coyotes I whipped.*

"But that's not important to . . ." she started to say until Scoot cut her off with a finger to her lips.

"Then I found out I own 320 acres of good land, a fixer-upper home and I have more money in the bank

111

than I've seen in one place my whole life," he finished.

Ruby was dumbfounded. "Fizz would fight a grizzly for me?" She laughed at the puzzled look on Scoot's face. "Of course I'll marry you. And, anybody that knows Scoot Merritt also knows the only person who thinks you're not worth a plug nickel is you.

"Besides, I know for a fact Fizz would take on a rat for you." Fizz sat up and cocked his head to one side then the next. Suddenly they remembered there was a cook shack full of listening ears when everyone broke into spontaneous applause.

Tink yelled, "Kiss her ya fool." Scoot obliged.

- - # - -

*Howdy, Journal: July 31*
      *I asked Ruby to marry me and she said, "Yes."*
*You could have knocked me over with a feather. Bein'*
*engaged don't feel like I thought it would. I've ribbed*
*more than one married cowboy about the ol' ball and*
*chain. Instead of feeling hobbled, suddenly I'm at 20,000*
*feet and the whole world is below me.*

# TWENTY-FOUR
## GETTIN' HITCHED

Ruby's Lake, Scoot's name for their favorite fishing hole became the backdrop for the wedding. A light breeze, cooled by the lake, fluttered the leaves on the trees. Small patches of clouds in an iridescent sky made random shade and then moved on. T.F. managed to get his chuck wagon there and served a Dutch oven meal with champagne and reception tent.

Then Scoot, Ruby and Fizz arrived in a black surrey pulled by a matched team of black and white Paint horses. Dozens of friends and relatives from both sides, plus some of the neighbors, showed up. T.F. tried to sound put out by all the freeloaders, but he wasn't very convincing. Pastor Colter gave the sermon and pronounced them cowboy and missus. Then Ruby read a poem that she had written titled "The Journey."

> *We've walked different paths,*
> *Crisscrossing Earth's extremities,*
> *Only to recognize in a face unknown,*

*Someone from the eternities.*
*Old friends. New love.*

     Instead of the customary stuffing of wedding cake in each other faces, Scoot and Ruby cast out their fishing lines, tangled them up on purpose, then kissed each other long enough that they both had to catch their breaths. Even T.F. could be heard sniffling. Fizz slicked up the leftovers and barely made the jump into the carriage. The Aussie seemed to know that something had changed in a very good way.

     The newlywed Merritts didn't have to stow away dozens of blenders, toasters, dishtowels and the like, to be dealt with after the honeymoon. They asked for nothing but fishing gear. Then under a hail of oats instead of rice, with poles and tackle packed, they departed for Coeur d'Alene, Idaho to spend their first three nights.

     From there, they fished their way up the Selway and Lochsa River. Next came Kelly Creek on into the North Fork of the Clearwater. St. Joe River took them further into the panhandle. The plan was to spend three days on the St. Joe, until they remembered Henry's Fork on the Snake River. That was their next stop.

     On their return from Henry's, they began planning the stops that needed to be made before going home. Scoot added one more.

     "We have to stop at the rest home. George is expecting us."

## TWENTY-FIVE
### HEROES CAN'T BE ANYTHING BUT HEROES

The backlit figure paced in front of the windowed wall that looked out onto the parking lot of the nursing home. Scoot wore a look of guilt mixed with apprehension as he glanced nervously at the door leading out into the hallway. It had been too long since his last visit. Soon a nurse would be wheeling in the man that had been as much of a father to him as his own. George Wilmer gave Scoot his first job while he was still in high school and wanting to be a cowboy more than anything in the world. School had never appealed to Scoot; the world outside of those walls kept calling him like the sirens in Homer's *Iliad*. George took him under his wing, after a considerable amount of Edna's good-humored nagging and as a favor to their friends, Scoot's grandparents. George had given him his nickname.

"The first, and maybe only rule I have on this place," he said, "is that when I holler for something to be done, you better scoot, youngster, because it may be the

115

difference between not gettin' kilt or having my foot up your backside."

Scoot worked hard, got shown the ropes by some of the best hands at the spread, and found a mentor and a friend in the owner of Lark Springs Ranch.

Now Scoot was fearful to see what remained of his friend after 83 years of living and the ravages of Alzheimer's. George's downward spiral began after Edna's death and the diagnosis of the fearsome disease. Scoot's visits became sporadic as George withdrew into himself. Scoot hadn't returned for almost a year.

Kitty, George and Edna's oldest, could be heard talking to the nurse as they came down the hall. Scoot stepped to Ruby's side, took off his hat and held it in both hands while Ruby put her arm around his waist. She felt him shivering and rubbed his back. The wind left his lungs at first sight of the blanket-wrapped figure, listing slightly to the right side of the wheelchair with his chin resting on his chest. Kitty tiptoed over to wrap Scoot and Ruby up in one big hug.

"It may not seem like it, but I know he's glad you're both here," she whispered. The nurse set the brakes on the chair, smiled and said, "I'll be down the hall."

Ruby slid a chair next to George, sat down and tenderly slipped her left arm around his frail shoulders. She took his right hand into hers and quietly introduced herself. "Mr. Wilmer, I'm Ruby Merritt, Scoot's wife. I'm honored to meet you. I know how much my husband loves you and Edna, and I've been looking forward to the time when I could thank you for being one of the people that made my husband the good man he is.

"We've just returned from our honeymoon where we fished clear up through Idaho almost to the Canadian border. Scoot has been dying to tell you about it but he's also been afraid to come," she said, looking at her husband. "Like most people, we want to keep our memories all shined up and new. We don't want our heroes to be anything other than heroes.

"Anyway, I'm taking up Scoot's visiting time and I know he has a lot to say. Goodbye, Mr. Wilmer." She softly kissed him on the forehead, walked over and hugged Scoot then went out into the hallway with Kitty.

Scoot watched the two women until they were out of sight, glanced at George then down at his own hat. After a few moments, he took a deep breath and sat next to his friend.

"Ain't she something, George? She reminds me so much of Edna, always knowing what to say and what people are thinking. I've never met anyone that doesn't like her, and I knew you would take to her right off.

"You remember how I'd rather sit on a hot branding iron than talk to folks, but danged if I don't want the day to hurry and get over so's I can be with her. She's got that mutt Fizz so wrapped around her little finger that he looks more lovesick than I do. "Aww, George, I'm so sorry I ain't been to see you for a bit. Maybe I was hoping if I stayed away things'd never change. That one day you would just show up at the ranch and everything would be like before. Edna would

117

step out the front door and wave to us with the dishcloth like she always did.

"We're gettin' ready for the fall gather and branding. Sure wish you'd come and help us out, even if was ta just make coffee like always. A cup of George's java to get the blood circulatin', ya know, that morning kick in the pants.

"Heck, who are we fooling, George? You made the worst coffee on God's green earth. The boys and me joked about having to suck on a horse turd just to get the taste out of our mouths. Remember you used to say, 'When you can stand a horseshoe up in it, it's ready.' Dang it, George, even if you dropped the whole horse in, the critter would dissolve before it hit bottom." Scoot laughed.

"I stopped by the old place, on the way back from the honeymoon, and ya know, your kids and grandkids are sure doing a good job with it. Heck, there's even great grandkids. That little Lilly, she's three now. She calls Lyle grandpa and you're grandpapa. She wonders why you can't talk to her and hold her on your lap so Kitty tells her that you miss Grandmama Edna so much that you ain't got time for nothing else."

Scoot placed his hand over George's. "I miss you old friend, but like Ruby said, I can't bear to see you this way. You'll always be George Wilmer, sitting on that big black gelding of yours. That was one cow eatin', ground covering horse.

"Remember when old H. Jackson Foster's cows would tear down the fences and get over onto your place and you'd take after them like a banshee screamin', 'You H. Jackson sonsabucks, I'm gonna send you back to hell!'" Scoot rubbed a rough hand across his eyes and straightened up when he heard Ruby and Kitty walk in with the nurse.

"I'm sorry to break into the visit so soon, but we need to get Mr. Wilmer cleaned up and ready for bed," the nurse said.

Scoot stood up, still holding George's hand. "I promise we'll get by sooner next time." He started to let go of the limp hand but it tightened onto his. He turned and squatted down in front of George so he could look into the old man's face. Their gaze met and Scoot noticed the blue return to George's eyes. That summer sky blue that always settled onto the horizon above the ranch. The same blue that blazed as the years vanished off his face every time George climbed into the saddle. Then he would move out across the dew-covered sage on those crisp mornings just before the sun topped the far hills. It telegraphed a silent message between the two friends. Scoot pressed his cheek to the old man's ear. "Goodbye, George. Give Edna my love - - and tell her about Ruby."

Before they dozed off that evening, Ruby held Scoot tightly as he talked about his life at Lark Springs. Then he dreamt that he was back on Lark Springs Ranch. It sparkled like there had been a good rain the night before and everything smelled fresh and new.

Scoot noticed a gauntlet of cowboys, cattle, horses and dogs. He walked over to ask one of the men what was going on but the man just raised a finger to his lips. Then the dogs started whimpering and looking in the direction of the old homestead. He turned and saw George walking towards the opening. Everyone snapped to attention - animals, people, everyone.

"I got your horse brushed and saddled for ya. He shines like a new penny."

At the end of the two rows of man and beast, there stood the black horse, neck arched, pawing the ground the way he always did when he wanted to get to work.

"Hey, where ya headed, George? Can I come?" Suddenly Scoot realized that he was still that wet-behind-the-ears kid.

George put his hand on Scoot's shoulder. "No son, but you take good care of that gal Ruby, she's a keeper."

George walked towards his horse, stopping to rub the heads of some of the cattle and other horses, talk to the dogs and shake hands with his friends. In the distance Edna waved with a dishcloth. George swung up into the saddle, and with a final salute, turned the horse and loped towards her.

Scoot was watching tears make dots in the dust on his boots when the phone beside the bed rang. The alarm clock glowed 2:10. It was Kitty calling to say that George had died. Then she chuckled as she related how the night staff had come a running when they heard George yelling, "You H. Jackson sonsabucks, I'm going to send you back to hell!"

# TWENTY-SIX
## WE'RE GONNA MAKE A RUN FOR IT!

"A cat? What do you mean you've got a cat? You never told me you had a cat," Scoot ranted. "I'm coming here to meet your family, not some mangy critter. What's next? You're all a coven of witches?"

Scoot had Fizz's attention. *Cat? Not on my watch!*

"He's not mangy and we're not witches." Ruby laughed. "Besides, you told me you loved everything about me, and that should include my cat." She laid her head on his shoulder and ran a finger up his arm.

"If you had read the small print you'd know that 'everything' does not include cats or ex-boyfriends."

Scoot turned the truck into the drive just past the mailbox with "The Evans" painted on it. A white wood-frame house with blue shutters and a detached garage sat in the shade of a giant willow and several cottonwood trees. The neatly kept yard had flowers in boxes that lined the front porch and a vegetable garden to the side

121

reminded him of a postcard from the 1950's. Cars and trucks were so jammed in the drive and along the fence that only one space remained for the newly weds.

Scoot smiled. "You'd think they were expecting somebody."

Before he had even put the Ford in park, the front door of the house flew open and people spilled out onto the porch and down the stairs, most with arms outstretched. "Close the door! We're gonna make a run for it," Scoot whispered, just as Ruby reached over and took the keys out of the ignition.

"Oh no, you don't. We're facing them together. That means you too, Fizz."

Amidst all of the handshakes, hugs and kisses, Scoot watched Fizz get scooped up by a bunch of kids and hauled off to the back yard. The dog squirmed to get away until someone stuffed a cookie in his face.

As if on command, the mass of humanity reversed direction and was sucked back into the house with the couple in tow. Scoot was trying to put names to faces when a large, work-worn hand emerged from the crowd, grasped Scoot's and steered him toward the front door.

"I'm Koz Evans, Ruby's grandpa. Let's slip outta this hen house and sit on the porch. I love my family, just in smaller chunks."

"Thanks, Mr. Evans. I was startin' to feel like I'd been caught in a stampede."

"Please, it's either Koz or Your Royal Highness. You chose."

"Koz it is, then."

Once they had settled into a pair of rockers, Koz slid his chair closer to Scoot. "How was the fishing, son? Ruby's my fishing buddy and we would talk about all the 'what if' places we'd go when there was time. Of course, time is a rare commodity these days."

"She had it all planned out, Koz. Every spot marked on the map, even down to the time of day when the fish were biting. She's a walking encyclopedia. Ruby can name a fish by the sound of its splash."

"I promised myself when I retired you couldn't drag me off a stream with a team of horses. Nowadays, my eyes are like looking through dirty water and knees feel like rusty hinges. My veterinarian keeps telling me I'm getting old. Doctors. What does that bunch of idiots know anyway?"

"Mr. Evans, you got any good fishing around here? Ain't no reason I couldn't tell you about our trip sittin' next to the water with a couple poles, is there?"

The old man patted Scoot's arm. "Welcome to the family."

Ruby emerged from the house with a twenty-pound ball of fur in her arms. "This is my cat, Fractious. Are you two going to get along or do you need a talkin' to?"

"All right. If he won't use my hat for a litter box, I won't shoot 'im. How's that for a treaty?"

"That'll do for now." Ruby smiled and went back into the house.

123

Koz watched the screen door close. "I don't know why God created cats. Mosquitoes are vexation enough."

"I'm going to enjoy being kin, Your Royal Highness."

The meal was down-home and as noisy as Scoot had ever experienced. He answered questions between mouthfuls of fried chicken, potato salad, corn-on-the-cob and hot biscuits. Every embarrassing moment in Ruby's life had to be replayed. Scoot had wanted to take notes until Ruby gave him "that look."

Once the dinner dishes were cleared and the rest of the family had either gone home or settled into the lawn chairs in the back yard, Koz and Scoot slipped away. They found a shady spot next to a little eddy in the local stream. The two sat without talking to let the sounds and smells wash over them at the winding down of the day.

"Ya got a great family, Koz. Seems like this has always been home."

"Yup. Except for two years during the Korean War. I swore if I made it home alive, I'd never leave. Sometimes I wish I hadn't made that promise."

Scoot twisted in his chair. "I've done nothing but bounce around since I left home. You've been a schoolteacher, farmer, mayor, and coach. I can't imagine you, of all people, havin' regrets."

"If you'd stayed put, would you have met Ruby?"

Scoot looked stunned. He watched the water slip over and between the rocks. "Koz, I took a train into the Canadian Rockies and went to places where the quiet is a thousand years old. Lake Elizabeth, in Great Basin Park, is an unearthly blue with corpses of huge trees resting just under the surface.

"I sat on a horse and looked out across Judith Basin in Montana knowing I'd covered some of the same country Charlie Russell had. I got so hypnotized by the waves coming into Cape Arago on the Oregon coast that the sun began to drop into the ocean 'fore I came out of the trance.

Scoot pointed at the stream. "The flash of a steelhead just before it takes my fly like a torpedo and then bends the pole double is somethin' every fisherman dreams about. I've seen it first-hand.

"There are vistas at the Grand Canyon that'll stop your heart, Koz. I sat in a Navajo hogan and listened to histories that had been passed from father to son so many times there's no way of knowin' the beginning. There's so much livin' to be done.

"But ya know what, Mr. Evans? None of it compares to watching Ruby sleep as the dawn starts lighting up the room. I can pick her laugh out of a crowd and I've seen a child's tears dry up with just one word from her. There's nothin' like it."

"Young man, we weren't handed an itinerary when we came into this world, and all that's leaving with us is memories. You've seen and done more in 29 years than most people have in 80. And it's been *your* choosing. Few people have the will or the backbone to do that."

125

Sitting up in his chair, he leaned closer to the cowboy. "We've only known each other for a few hours, Scoot, but I see in you a young me, only you're going for the brass ring. I've heard the admiration in people's voices for the life that you're living, and I've also heard the 'Aw shucks, pardner, it ain't nothin' BS.

"You're no dummy. There's a depth and an intellect you're hiding, and I can't figure why. But whatever the reason, you have a gift and the opportunity to help people like me see the world through your eyes."

A silence fell between the two. Scoot sat with his mouth hanging open like the flap in Grandpa's long johns.

"You're right, Koz. Dang it, you're right. Ruby's been like a splash of cold water, lettin' me know there's something in me that needs to either be chased or left buried."

*Cannon balllll!* A furry black and white flash shot between the two and dove into the stream at their feet.

"Thanks, Fizz." Scoot chuckled. "So much for the fishin'."

Koz smiled. "That's not why we came here anyway, was it?"

Ruby wiped her eyes, then walked over and wrapped Scoot in a hug from behind, kissing his neck.

"Hey, Darlin', how long you two been here?"

"Long enough," she whispered.

## TWENTY-SEVEN
### EAT LIZARD!

The newlyweds visited with Koz and Edith Evans late into the night. Scoot felt like he had been drawn into a circle. He once wrote that he "would know when it was time to roost." It was time.

Goodbyes were heartfelt and difficult. Even Fizz had to be told to get in the truck. He looked up at Ruby's grandparents, then the Red F-250. *You two keep the cat; I've got a better gig.* When Scoot put his hands on his hips, the dog walked slowly and reluctantly off the porch. Fractious growled at Fizz from his pet carrier when he finally jumped into the back. Fizz flopped onto the seat. *I'm riding shotgun, hairball.*

Scoot and Ruby talked through the remainder of the night at the motel. Bleary-eyed, they returned to the ranch to let T.F. know of their plans. The couple intended to take up residence in the house on Scoot's land. They bought Zip, the horse, and packed Scoot's belongings.

"You've got a bookcase full of those sketch books you're always packing around," Ruby exclaimed. "This is the big secret you've been keeping?"

She gasped when she leafed through the pages. "Scoot, these are your illustrated memoirs. They're beautiful!"

"Naw," he said, doubtfully. "Just a few coloring books with some scratchings."

"Coloring books? These are treasures!"

He quickly grabbed the one labeled 'Ruby.' "No peeking at this one, it's not finished."

Several boxes and a couple hours later, Scoot's worldly belongings sat on the bed of their truck. Ruby glanced at the load then at her husband. "You travel light."

"A feller never knows when he might have ta git outta town ahead of the sheriff."

Scoot gave Ruby a piggyback ride to the cook shack for their final meal at Sprocket Ranch. Everyone stayed to talk about pranks, rats and fishing. T.F. finally broke it up.

"We can't afford to loiter. There's too much work and not enough day. Besides, you two are fired. Go get on with your lives." Scoot shook hands, Ruby hugged and Fizz checked under the tables for scraps.

The truck and trailer pulled slowly out of the yard toward the main gate. Mr. and Mrs. Sprocket and crew waved from the porch.

Fizz stood with his front paws over the seat and watched everything recede until dust from the truck and trailer clouded his view. *We got the cook, you have to eat lizard.*

- - # - -

*Howdy, Journal: A new page*
*We left Sprocket Ranch with all my belongings. I don't remember any other outfits that were as hard to pull away from. Ruby felt it, too. She hugged my arm and wiped her eyes on my shirt. Fizz watched out the window 'til he couldn't see 'em no more.*

G. L. Rasmussen

# TWENTY-EIGHT
## I'VE GOT SOMETHING FOR YOU

They had begun remodeling the two-story wood-frame house right after they moved in when Ruby walked into the upstairs bedroom. Scoot was covered with drywall dust. Fractious and Fizz sat in the doorway observing the odd ritual.

Ruby searched for a clean spot on his face to kiss, but gave up. "I'm going to have to hang you on the clothes line and beat you like a rug! You'll get a kiss after you shower. Oh, everything on your list is downstairs, except the rest of the sheet rock and lumber. Conklin's said they could deliver it first thing in the morning."

"Thank you." He noticed the Cheshire cat-sized grin on her face reflected in the window. "What?"

"I've got something for you. Remember my friend, Alisha, from the wedding? I showed her one of your books."

Scoot spun around. "Why? You're the only one that's seen 'em, Ruby. I didn't make them for everybody to gawk at! Not yet, anyways." He turned and leaned against the window. Ruby stuck an envelope in front of his face.

"Before you open it, you should know that Alisha is an editor for Bettencourt Publishing. She ran your book past the 'new authors' panel."

"What . . . did they think?"

"Let the money do the talking. There's a check and a contract inside."

The dust-covered cowboy looked in the envelope and then closed it. "That's a lot of zeros."

Ruby screamed and did a little dance. Fizz and Fractious ran downstairs and ducked behind the couch.

Fizz glowered at the cat. *You crapped in his hat again, didn't you, hairball?*


- - # - -


*Howdy, Journal: Yeehaa!*

*I'm an author. Some big city fools think these scratchins' might be worth something. Ruby said, "I told you so." Bettencourt Publishing even gave me a $10,000 advance ta see if the rest of the world agrees. Scoot Merritt's life will be out there for anybody with twenty bucks. Kinda scary.*

# TWENTY-NINE
## DON'T KEEP T. F. WAITIN'

Part of being a published author involved book signings and promotional tours. Although Ruby and Fizz seemed to enjoy the attention, Scoot didn't. Except for the times when Ruby took him to fish places that they had only dreamt about. Scoot's list of great fishing holes now included everything from Alaska to Florida.

Their favorite signing event was at Elko, Nevada.

"You're costing me money, Bill Shakespeare. This book better be good." Scoot was writing on an inside cover when he heard T.F.'s voice. Sprocket Ranch had shut down for the day and the grinning crew stood in line.

Scoot jumped onto the table. "Everyone, I want you to meet the characters from my book." A cheer and applause went up from the crowd.

The Sprocket bunch clearly relished their moment of fame. T.F. even signed autographs, stood without complaint for pictures and smiled when he had his

133

behind patted by more than one female fan. There was a Tink-sized hole in the festivities, though.

Rancher Sprocket even sprung for dinner at a local steak house. Everyone had ideas for Scoot's next book. Bronc figured a book about himself would be a hot seller.

"Tink went back to Arizona and took Amy on a second honeymoon. Now she's feathering the nest for their young'un." T.F. looked around the table. Matt and Cody Clegg each had a girl friend sporting an engagement ring. Bronc's wife, Cassie, was packing a new baby. "I've decided to hire eunuchs from now on. Like the Buck's."

"I ain't eunuch, I'm Presbyterian."

"That means you'd be singing soprano in the choir," Buck Harmstead clarified.

"Oh. OH!" His eyebrows scrunched and eyes narrowed. "Is that gonna be retroactive?"

The group visited and hurrahed each other until the restaurant manager finally convinced them that thirty minutes past closing time was their limit. When T.F. dropped a hundred dollar bill on the table as a tip, the manager suddenly became all smiles.

"You're welcome back anytime, ladies and gentlemen," he gushed, rubbing his hands together.

While Sprocket Ranch and guests loaded into vehicles, T.F. pulled Ruby into his arms and slapped Scoot on the back.

"I've rarely had anybody tell me that my life was worth a lick. You wrote about me. Suddenly, folks figure

I'm worth knowin' and now I'm 'Mister Sprocket' and it's 'Yes sir, No sir.' I'll deny that I said this, but thank you."

He held his niece for a moment longer and then eased himself into the car with his wife. They pulled away from the curb to follow the others toward home. Later, T.F.'s wife said that was probably one of the last lucid moments Mr. Sprocket had. Dementia clouded his mind and a massive stroke knocked him off a ranch loading-chute.

Scoot and Ruby were in L.A. at a writer's conference and awards ceremony when they got the call. They excused themselves and flew immediately to the hospital. Tiptoeing into the ICU, they squeezed T.F.'s wife's hand. When the couple approached his bedside, he motioned for them to lean closer and mouthed the words, "You're fired."

He lingered another three days. Long enough to see television and newspaper reports of his illness and life. Hundreds of get-well cards papered the hospital walls. Scoot was reading "90 Days in the Pen" to T.F. when Ruby softly laid her hand over her husband's and closed the book.

Family and friends gathered at his bedside and shared their favorite story about T.F. until early the next morning.

He was buried in the family cemetery at the ranch on a particularly hot August day. Hundreds crowded around, some with hats in hand, others with books he had signed. His tombstone read:

135

*Theodore Franklin Sprocket*
*Cowboy, Rancher, Husband, Friend.*
*Don't keep T.F. waiting, St. Peter,*
*you'll be hunting a new job*

The ranch was left to his wife, oldest son Frank the bean counter, and the two Bucks. Frank took over all of the financial affairs in a way that would have made his father proud. Buck Turnbow and Buck Harmstead co-managed the day-to-day operations.

- - # - -

*Howdy, Journal: August 17*
*Theodore Franklin Sprocket is gone. Couldn't write "dead." Maybe, "over the next ridge." I got ta see my old friend, George, in a dream just 'fore he rode off to his wife. Ain't had a visit from T.F., yet.*
*Tink, Amy and Benjamin, Jr. were at the funeral. We've kept in touch since then. Ruby and me have been wantin' to set 'em down and bounce an idea off the two. We've got our fingers crossed.*

# THIRTY
## SKINNIN' CATS

**L.A. Leader: Literary Section**

The success of "The Light on the Far Hills" book series is understandable. Scoot Merritt's plainspoken travelogues are fresh and engaging. His sketches and watercolors, reminiscent of early Charlie Russell, grace these literary treasures. Merritt can walk-the-walk and talk-the-talk and this is his life, unadorned, in his own words and art.

Tink glanced at Scoot and smiled. "Write-ups in major newspapers, TV and radio interviews! Who'd have thought this was the same driftin' bronc twister from Oregon with a mutt named Fizz and a beautiful wife that can shoot and fish as good as she can cook." He flipped through the rest of the binder. Several more sat on the shelf.

"Thank you for the well-deserved compliment," Ruby laughed and kissed Tink on the cheek. She handed Benjamin Jr. back to Amy and hurried to answer another phone. "You better watch your back though, Tink. Fizz understands people talk and knows what a mutt is." Fizz stared at Tink.

Scoot stood at the desk and divided his attention between two cell phones, one in each ear.

When the din finally quieted, Tink threw his hands in the air. "Are you guys crazy? Look at this disaster! You two can afford to build a two-story warehouse on the place. Doesn't have to be huge but it needs at least three nice offices and a conference room. Hire a full-time secretary for day-to-day and two part-time grunts for incoming and outgoing shipments. Please tell me there are accountants and lawyers on retainer."

"Yup," Scoot said, smiling. "You thinkin' we might need a business manager or something?"

"That's a place to start."

Scoot pulled a card out of the desk and handed it to Tink. "This is accounting's number. Give 'em your W-4 info and how much you're wantin' for a salary."

Tink stared at it. "Me?"

"Who else?" Scoot asked, grinning.

Tink glanced at Amy, who nodded. "Well . . . okay! I accept.

Scoot clapped his hands and looked at Ruby. "All right, we've skinned that cat. Let's talk profit sharing over a steak. Where are we goin' for dinner?"

A wife, a cat and a dog stared in stunned silence. "That's just a figure of speech. We ain't skinnin' no cats," he clarified.

The Aussie grin vanished. *Dang. Throw me a bone then take it away.*

# THIRTY-ONE
## KOZ GRABS THE BRASS RING

The Situk River originated in the mountains north of Yakutal. It flowed across a dab of Alaskan real estate, perched just over the border of the Yukon and British Columbia and eventually into the Gulf of Alaska. Fed from the Mountain and Situk Lakes, the river sliced through lush rain forest.

Within its waters could be found Dolly Varden, Char, and resident Rainbow Trout. Kenai, Sockeye, Pink and Silver Salmon also navigated upstream to spawn. And it laid claim to some of the finest Steelhead fishing in North America.

Twelve first-time Situk fisherman and two guides, Charlie and Bobber, made their way through dense undergrowth while Charlie rehearsed the history of the area.

"Steelhead run, on average, about twenty pounds, the record being forty two. Salmon are much larger, around fifty. The current record, a ninety-seven pounder,

139

was caught at Bell Island."

For Ruby, this was sacred ground. "We're here during prime Steelhead season. They'll start moving out when the Salmon move in."

"That's my walking encyclopedia," Koz said, chuckling. "My bet's on her to pull in the first one."

"I don't think you'll have any takers on that bet, Koz." Scoot squeezed Ruby's hand.

Also in the group were Ruby's two brothers and spouses, two sisters with their husbands and Scoot's father, Hugh.

Koz had been tutored by Ruby and Scoot. "For an old man," he said, "I can whip a fly around pretty good."

Koz Evans grabbed the brass ring at seventy-five on the Situk River. He landed a thirty-seven inch steelhead with his family as the cheering section. It was large enough for Koz to legally keep as a trophy mount. Instead, he kissed it on the head, quietly said "Thank You" and let it slip back into the Alaskan waters. The photos of him and "the monster" became his constant companion and were shown to anyone he could corner.

Ruby's Lake remained the favorite summer gathering place, though, for the Evans/Merritt clan. As the families grew, so did the number of lawn chairs at waters edge. Empty chairs were placed in honor of those that were there in memory only.

Sometimes the fish weren't biting, but that really wasn't why they were there.

# Thirty-two
## A beginning

Zip's breathing was even and steady while he and Scoot raced toward the edge of the butte. They had been gathering cattle, but for some reason, no one else had shown up to help. Then Scoot had the feeling that Ruby needed him.

The Paint gelding gathered himself and leapt off the horizontal top onto the steep slope. Scoot lay back in the saddle and kicked the stirrups forward. Zip nearly sat on his hindquarters as he slid on the loose footing of the side hill. A length from the base, he pushed off, landed on the desert floor and was in full stride in moments.

Some cattle, bunched around a stream, scattered and crashed into each other in an attempt to get out of the horse and rider's way. Scoot leaned forward, coaxing his mount on.

The few undulations in the landscape gave way to level ground and then a white frame house appeared like a dot on the horizon. Zip moved easily, gliding between the sagebrush and around the Joshua trees. He stretched

141

out even further, reaching deep down inside. The landscape became a blur and the brim of Scoot's hat flattened against the crown. Zip's breathing and the wind were the only sounds.

Topping a small rise, a cheering Sprocket crew came into sight, waving their hats.

"What are they doin' standin' around when there's work to do?" he wondered out loud.

Even at Zip's blinding speed, Scoot could make out their faces clearly. Time slowed and in his mind he clicked off each one. There's the Clegg brothers, grinning like always. Bronc sat off to the side, giving Scoot directions while the two Bucks, sitting astride their horses, looked like they were born a'horseback and hoped to die there. With arms crossed, Tink leaned over the saddlehorn. Wil sat an ATV next to him. "My horses gotta have wheels," he always said.

Scoot tipped his hat. Looking up the trail, he saw his folks, grandparents, Ruby's family, George and Edna and three children he didn't recognize, yet seemed to know. T.F. stood apart from the others, smiling and pointing at his kilt. Scoot was half-tempted to turn around and give T.F. a hard time.

The white frame home loomed and as the horse slid to a stop, its rider jumped off and ran through the open door. Fizz barked and Fractious surveyed a paw.

Dusting himself off, Scoot stepped into the all white sunlit room. Ruby lay in the bed and cradled a blanketed bundle.

A doctor slapped Scoot on the shoulder as he left the room. "They're all healthy. Congratulations, Dad."

"They? There's more than one?" He glanced between the doctor and Ruby. She patted the bed, motioning for him to sit beside her. Then she opened the blanket. Four little Fractiouses peeked out.

*Kittens? I'm the father of kittens?* Scoot sat up, struggling to get out of the dream. *I've gotta quit eating pizza late at night.* He rubbed his eyes, trying to get them to focus.

Ruby was awake and smiling, posed like Cleopatra on the royal barge. "I know something you don't know."

Scoot yawned. "I hope it don't have anything to do with kittens."

THE END

## G. L. Rasmussen

ABOUT THE AUTHOR

Gary is originally from Northern Utah, born and raised in the Bear River Valley. He spent his summers working on the family farm, for local farmers and ranchers or horseback.

Offered scholarships in Agriculture and Advertising Design, he opted for the bright lights and big city. Eight years in the advertising field convinced him that wasn't where he wanted to be. Gary has also worked as a ranch manager, cowboy, pen rider, horse trainer, newspaper columnist, graphic designer and illustrator. He's active in the Idaho Writers League and is a former president of the Western Art Guild.

Gary has traveled extensively throughout Europe, Great Britain and the United States. He and Margie reside in Twin Falls, Idaho and are the parents of four children and nine grandchildren.